What Reviews Books

"With its expected u... ... and healthy dose of humor, *Blind* ... ...at will keep you guessing." – *Bay Wind...*

"In a succinct film style ...ve, with scenes that move, a character-driven plot, and crisp dialogue worthy of a screenplay ... the Richfield and Rivers novels are ... an engaging Hollywood mystery ... series." – *Midwest Book Review*

Force of Nature "...is filled with nonstop, fast paced action. Tornadoes, raging fire blazes, heroic and daring rescues... Baldwin does a fine job of describing the fast-paced scenes and inspiring the reader to keep on turning the pages." – *L-word.comLiterature*

In the Jude Devine mystery series the "...characters seem fully capable of walking away from the particulars of whodunit and engaging the reader in other aspects of their lives." – *Lambda Book Report*

Mine "...weaves a tale of yearning, love, lust, and conflict resolution ... a believable plot, with strong characters in a charming setting." – *JustAboutWrite*

"While these two women struggle with their issues, there is some very, very hot sex. If you enjoy complex characters and passionate sex scenes, you'll love *Wild Abandon*." – *MegaScene*

"*Course of Action* is a romance ... populated with a host of captivating and amiable characters. The glimpses into the lifestyles of the rich and beautiful people are rather like guilty pleasures ... a most satisfying and entertaining reading experience." – *Midwest Book Review*

The Clinic is "...a spellbinding novel." – *JustAboutWrite*

"*Unexpected Sparks* lived up to its promise and was thoroughly enjoyable ... Dartt did a lovely job at building the relationship between Kate and Nikki." – *Lambda Book Report*

"*Sequestered Hearts* ... is everything a romance should be. It is teeming with longing, heartbreak, and of course, love. As pure romances go, it is one of the best in print today." – *L-word.comLiterature*

"*The Exile and the Sorcerer* is a mesmerizing read, a tour-de-force packed with adventure, ordeals, complex twists and turns, and the internal introspection of appealing characters." – *Midwest Book Review*

The Spanish Pearl is "...both science fiction and romance in this adventurous tale ... A most entertaining read, with a sequel already in the works. Hot, hot, hot!" – *Minnesota Literature*

"A deliciously sexy thriller ... *Dark Valentine* is funny, scary, and very realistic. The story is tightly written and keeps the reader gripped to the exciting end." – *JustAbout Write*

"*Punk Like Me* ... is different. It is engaging. It is life-affirming. Frankly, it is genius. This is a rare book in that it has a soul; one that is laid bare for all to see." – *JustAboutWrite*

"*Chance* is not a novel about the music industry; it is about a woman discovering herself as she muddles through all the trappings of fame." – *Midwest Book Review*

Sweet Creek "... is sublimely in tune with the times." – *Q-Syndicate*

"*Forever Found* ... neatly combines hot sex scenes, humor, engaging characters, and an exciting story." – *MegaScene*

Shield of Justice is a "...well-plotted...lovely romance...I couldn't turn the pages fast enough!" – Ann Bannon, author of *The Beebo Brinker Chronicles*

The 100th Generation is "...filled with ancient myths, Egyptian gods and goddesses, legends, and, most wonderfully, it contains the lesbian equivalent of Indiana Jones living and working in modern Egypt." – *Just About Write*

Sword of the Guardian is "...a terrific adventure, coming of age story, a romance, and tale of courtly intrigue, attempted assassination, and gender confusion ... a rollicking fun book and a must-read for those who enjoy courtly light fantasy in a medieval-seeming time." – *Midwest Book Review*

"*Of Drag Kings and the Wheel of Fate*'s lush rush of a romance incorporates reincarnation, a grounded transman and his peppy daughter, and the dark moods of a troubled witch—wonderful homage to Leslie Feinberg's classic gender-bending novel, *Stone Butch Blues*." – *Q-Syndicate*

In *Running with the Wind* "...the discussions of the nature of sex, love, power, and sexuality are insightful and represent a welcome voice from the view of late-20-something characters today." – *Midwest Book Review*

"Rich in character portrayal, *The Devil Inside* is an unusual, unpredictable, and thought-provoking love story that will have the reader questioning the definition of right and wrong long after she finishes the book." – *JustAboutWrite*

Wall of Silence "...is perfectly plotted and has a very real voice and consistently accurate tone, which is not always the case with lesbian mysteries." – *Midwest Book Review*

SPLIT
THE
ACES

by

Jove Belle

2008

SPLIT THE ACES

ISBN 10: 1-60282-033-3
ISBN 13: 978-1-60282-033-3

This Trade Paperback Original Is Published By
Bold Strokes Books, Inc.
New York, USA

First Edition: October 2008

CREDITS
EDITOR: JENNIFER KNIGHT
PRODUCTION DESIGN: STACIA SEAMAN
COVER DESIGN BY SHERI (GRAPHICARTIST2020@HOTMAIL.COM)

Acknowledgments

My heartfelt gratitude to Len Barot for having the vision and business savvy to make Bold Strokes the coolest ticket in town. I'm especially grateful that you invited me along for the ride. What a rush.

Thanks to Jennifer Knight for ironing the bumps out of the road. The depth of your knowledge never fails to amaze me. In a pinch, I'm betting on 17 black.

Michelle, keep growing, you'll get there. Thanks for saving my schedule-impaired ass time and time again.

Tara, thank you for thirteen years, three gray-hair-inducing children, and the never-failing support. Without you, I'd still be searching for home and there would be no room in my heart for writing.

Finally, to all my friends, thank you for pitching in for daycare during the crunch times. I love you guys in spite of your questionable judgment.

By the Author

Edge of Darkness

Split the Aces

Dedication

For Tara – you are my true north.

CHAPTER ONE

She had thirty minutes till she had to be back behind her blackjack table, and Rae Sutherland wanted to get laid.

She also wanted to smoke, but the Camel would still be an option later when she went on her fifteen-minute break. The five feet five inches of Midwest farmer's daughter leaning against the slots might not. They'd spent the last two hours circling each other, the woman moving to Rae's table and away again. The teasing promise never left her baby blue eyes. It was time to find out if she would deliver or run away.

Rae cut through the crowd, stopped well within the blonde's personal space, and claimed her hand. Without so much as a hello, she led her off the casino floor.

"Where are we going?" the woman asked.

Rae didn't slow her pace. She cast a sideways glance at her intended "date," letting her eyes fill with as much sex and heat as she could manage. The blonde's small gasp made her smile. Her message had been received loud and clear.

"In here." She ushered her new playmate into a storage room full of retired gaming machines, a graveyard of old Vegas that seemed to thrill her "guests." She locked the door and backed the woman against a tall slot machine. "We need to be quiet."

Urgent fingers fumbled with the studs holding Rae's shirt together. "Don't you want to know my name?"

Not really. Rae pushed the blonde's collar open and bit the soft skin where her neck blended into her shoulder, not hard, just enough to transmit intent. Moving her lips up, she murmured in her ear, "Sure, tell me."

She wouldn't remember but that was beside the point.

"Deb."

Tonight's hot snack crushed her mouth against Rae's in a sudden, forceful invasion that left her spinning. God, she wanted this woman. Naked. Now. She controlled the kiss, drawing Deb in, then surging forward, sliding her tongue into the welcoming warmth. Deb sucked hard and bit down lightly. The sharp edge of teeth shot pure fire to Rae's belly. Deb wasn't nearly as sweet as her shy, flirtatious glances across the casino had implied.

She broke free before Rae was ready, leaving Rae off balance, chasing after those teasing lips. Before she could reclaim Deb's mouth, she was brought up short by a pair of hands on her breasts. Deb squeezed and twisted her nipples, jarring her to the tightrope fine line between pain and desire. Rae felt the moan building in her chest.

"God, how do I get this open?" Deb asked with a growl. She wrapped her hands around Rae's lapels, the fine onyx studs forgotten as she jerked hard to open the front.

Rae gripped her wrists, holding her firm. "I have to go back to work in a minute." She barely managed to get the words out.

"Right." Deb's smoldering look was colored with disappointment and urgency.

She dropped to her knees, tugged open Rae's fly, and pushed her pants and underwear down her legs. A trail of bumps rose in the wake of her fingers. Rae was accustomed to being the one in charge but variety worked for her. She didn't object when Deb's smooth tongue found her aching clit.

This was the moment—the few intense seconds between possibility and *Oh, my God, this is really happening*—that kept Rae chasing down new women night after night. All thought fell away as her muscles began the hot dance toward release. When the doorknob rattled, she froze for a second and they stared at each other. Technically, Rae was off the clock, but she didn't want to be caught with her pants around her ankles and a casino guest on her knees in front of her. That would require too much explanation to her boss, and Rae didn't want to provide any extra fodder for his fantasies.

Deb's evil smile of challenge made her nervous. The smart thing to do was obvious. Whoever was rattling the door had given up but they would be back. She should get out now, while she could. Instead, she said, "Hurry."

Deb wrapped her lips around Rae's clit, her tongue pressed flat against it, and sucked. Hard. Rae squeezed her eyes shut, blocking out everything but the wet pulse of need. The encounter wasn't tender and romantic, but the throbbing beat coursing through her body demanded release. She locked her knees, willing herself to stay upright. Pinpoints of light formed in the blackness behind her closed eyelids.

"Christ." She gripped the slot machine with one hand, using the cold steel to ground herself. Her other hand found traction in Deb's hair, holding tight as she felt her body coil for release.

Deb's tongue beat a pounding, escalating rhythm that coursed through her until she overflowed. The orgasm skittered through her like a chain of firecrackers, and if not for Deb's hands around her hips, holding her firm, she would have fallen to the floor in a quivering heap.

"God-fucking-damn." She wanted to curl up and sleep,

chain smoke a pack of Camels, and slam back a triple shot of tequila. All at once. Instead she urged Deb upright with a not so gentle tug on her hair. "My turn."

She spun the blonde around and pushed in close, trapping her against the unforgiving, smooth glass of the slot machine. Deb struggled, turning her head to the side, her face a mix of shock and lust. Bursts of steam clouded the surface as she gulped air, quiet. Waiting.

Rae cupped the tight breasts, feeling the nipples straining through the layers of fabric as she ground her hips against Deb's ass. It was a great ass, round, firm, begging to be spanked. Rae wished she had all day to devote to worshiping it, making it shine red as she rode Deb hard. She'd have made her wait, made her plead. She glanced at her watch. Lunch was over in ten minutes. Not nearly enough time to do all she wanted.

She squeezed Deb's nipples, building to a hard crescendo, then scraped her nails down Deb's sides, digging in firmly enough to be felt through the layer of fabric.

"You've done this before." She punctuated her words with small nips to the back of Deb's neck, ending with her teeth clamped around the gasping blonde's ear. "A quick, hard fuck with your pants around your ankles, only a door to separate you from the party."

She could have been talking about her own sexual encounters over the past two years. She flicked open the top button of Deb's jeans. "Behind that innocent smile, that girl-next-door face, there's a woman like me who just…" She thrust against her and popped open another button. "…wants…" And another. "To fuck."

Rae skipped the rest of the buttons and forced her hand inside, over the thin barrier of Deb's cotton panties. She rounded Deb's clit and rubbed gently. "God, you're hard."

Deb pushed back in a slow grind, and Rae squeezed her

fingers down tight and milked the long edge of her desire, using the friction of the fabric to both mute and intensify the sensation. Sounds of casino life crowded in on them, urging them to hurry.

"Is this what you want?" Rae thrust her hips harder against Deb's ass. "To be fucked by a stranger?" She increased her tempo, tattooing a slower counter-rhythm against Deb's clit. "From behind? Pressed up against a wall? A door? An old slot machine?"

Deb strained against her. Rae could feel the beginning tremors of climax vibrating beneath her fingers. The loud clanging of somebody hitting the jackpot reached them as Deb tensed impossibly tight, shuddered, then sagged against her.

Rae flattened her hand, palming Deb's sex through her come-slicked panties. Her sexual partner's trembling, irregular twitching made her irrationally happy, as it always did. A glance at her watch told her she had only a few minutes to return to work. Barely enough time to wash her hands. Ready to be done with this encounter, she withdrew and backed away.

"I hate to run, but I have to get back to work."

Deb stared at her. "Really?" Her voice held a slight tremble.

What was it about tourists? It's like they thought she would be all of a twitter in the afterglow, so affected by imported pussy that she'd forget the things that really mattered, like her job.

"Yeah, really." Rae spoke softly, forcing herself to think of puppies and teddy bears. Hopefully that would make her sound nicer than she was, possibly even kind. She pulled up her pants and fastened them. "You can wait here for a few minutes if you want. Just lock the door when you're done."

She smoothed her hands over her shirt, straightened her tie, and gave her hair a flip. Her long, pale bangs settled low over her right eye. Without a backward glance, she unlocked the door and stepped out into the smoke-dimmed light of the gaming floor.

❖

Cori Romero smoothed her hands over the oil-slicked body sprawled across her massage table. The gentle trickle of water from a nearby fountain and the "Sounds of Nature" CD were intended to be calming, but her fingers tingled with energy.

She'd been expecting her regular Saturday afternoon client, Jeff Lindstrom, a man with enough hair on his back to carpet her entire office and then some. A few months ago, she'd offered the gentle hint that he should schedule a wax, but the big man only laughed and claimed he couldn't give up his pelt because his wife relied on him to keep her warm at night. Cori was sure there were other less hair-dependant ways he could achieve this goal, but she didn't mention them.

Now, with the wife in question, Patty, stretched out beneath her probing fingers, Cori knew Jeff was out of touch with what was really needed to keep her warm. He had called at the last minute to say he wouldn't be able to make it but Patty would keep the appointment in his place. The substitution was a pleasant surprise at the end of a crappy week.

Cori dug into a knot low in Patty's back. The taut skin was darker than her own olive complexion, through time spent in a tanning bed. Patty tensed beneath her insistent touch, then relaxed.

"Mmm, feels good." She shifted her hips slightly, pushing against Cori's hands.

Her sleepy murmur reminded Cori, with a jolt, of how long it'd been since she'd heard those words in a personal setting.

She forced herself to focus on decidedly unsexy images, like Jeff's hair-covered back. Of course, that led her thoughts along a winding trail to the very sexy, naked back of his wife.

She glanced at the clock on the wall, willing herself not to respond to the delicious temptation in front of her. Only ten more minutes of thinking clinical thoughts and her workday was over. Mentally, emotionally, she wasn't interested in the woman she was massaging. However, her body, specifically the growing wetness between her legs, didn't care if Patty was single, married, or scheduled to enter a convent at the end of the week. Cori squeezed her thighs together. She just had to keep it in her pants a little longer before she could escape to the safety of her apartment and indulge herself in a good book and the frothy pleasure of a tall latte. First, however, she'd need to change her underwear.

She shifted her thoughts to the coming week. She was leaving Wednesday for a massage convention in Las Vegas and wouldn't return until the following Monday. Maybe while she was there she would find an outlet for all her pent-up sexual energy. Casual affairs were not her usual style but, she had to admit, the possibility of an impromptu liaison in Sin City held a certain appeal. Why else would she have agreed to go? God knows, she wasn't interested in learning anything more about massage. Her career had long since lost its fascination for her.

Although she'd learned the science behind her massage technique in school, she still worked primarily by instinct, following tension through the muscles automatically. That's what led her hands over Patty's firmly muscled butt to the top of her thighs.

"You're really tense."

"I wonder why." Patty shifted her hips again, this time parting her legs slightly.

Cori jerked her hands away, flustered by the implication in Patty's voice. She knew she'd allowed the possibility to linger between them since their introduction an hour earlier. She'd enjoyed Patty's frank appraisal and obvious approval. Still, no matter how long it had been since she'd been with a woman, no amount of time was long enough for her to forget that Patty was straight. And married.

"Sorry." She covered Patty's body with the soft cotton sheet and patted her shoulder in what she hoped was a friendly, platonic sort of way. "Time's up."

As she moved toward the door, Patty grabbed her hand, halting her hasty retreat. "Wait." She sat up, letting the sheet pool around her waist. "You don't have to run away."

As much as Cori craved some excitement in her boring workaday routine, this was not what she had in mind. How was she supposed to gracefully turn down a woman who was clearly accustomed to getting what she wanted? Furthermore, did she really want to? There were no laws specifically prohibiting a sexual relationship between a massage therapist and her client, but technically Patty was paying for Cori's time. Being likened to a prostitute thudded in Cori's head, squashing the already-miniscule possibility of expanding the encounter.

"Mrs. Henderson," she said with intentional formality, reminding them both of her marital status, "I'm flattered but I have other obligations I must see to." It wasn't true, but the white lie was the safest way out of the room.

Patty's bottom lip turned down in a pout. "Really? Perhaps I could schedule an appointment for next Saturday? For a more *specialized* massage."

God, the woman was persistent. Cori wondered if she was giving off some sort of desperate-lesbian pheromones that attracted aggressive straight women.

"I'm going to be out of town next weekend." Her voice sounded disappointed even to her own ears.

Before Patty could respond, Cori thanked her for coming to Eden Body Works and bolted out the door and down the hall to the employee lounge. She carried with her a new determination to meet a woman to play with in Vegas, one who wasn't off-limits.

CHAPTER TWO

"Tell me we can stay here forever." Julie's voice held a pleading edge, like a child begging for a too-big serving of dessert.

Cori turned her head toward her friend and pried one eye open. "By the pool?" She shrugged. "Sure, why not?"

They'd arrived in Las Vegas less than two hours ago, barely taking the time to drop their bags in their shared room before heading to the pool. Compared to the constant gray of the overcast Seattle sky, the sun-drenched day was idyllic. The slate patio was awash with people in various states of undress, sprawled on loungers and posing around the pool. Cori studied the crowd, speculating about a few of the women, but she wasn't nearly brave enough to approach anyone. Perhaps a few more of the blended blue drinks that were served poolside would bolster her courage.

"My glass is empty," Julie said.

Cori sucked on her straw and confirmed that her drink was gone, too. "Don't you just hate that?" She pushed herself out of her lounger. It was Julie's turn to make the trip to the bar but she looked too comfortable to move. "I'll go."

"Mmm."

Cori took that as a thanks. She was almost to the bar when

a sporty dyke with dangerous blue eyes intercepted her, a drink in each hand.

"Looks like you need a refill," the stranger said.

Cori smiled, slightly disconcerted. "You must be a mind reader."

She mumbled an inward curse over her lame reply. If that was the best she could do when an attractive woman spoke to her, she should go back home now. She reached for the glasses, but the woman retreated slightly.

"I've got them." She offered up a cocky smile, full of practiced charm and self-assurance, and motioned toward Cori's vacant lounger. "I'll follow you."

It wasn't the first time a woman had bought her a drink, but it was broad daylight and they were outside, surrounded by a sea of presumably straight people. Being blatantly cruised under these circumstances caught Cori off guard.

"Thanks," she choked out as she tripped back to her chair.

The cocky stranger handed Julie her drink with a friendly, unassuming smile, and waited for Cori to be seated. Then she lowered herself onto the edge of Cori's lounger, close enough for the exposed thigh below the hem of her shorts to touch Cori's bare leg.

"I'm Rae." She held out her hand.

Cori's mouth went dry and she forgot how to talk. When Rae's smile broadened and she flicked her eyes down to the outstretched hand, Cori regained her basic motor functions. "Um, sorry. I'm Cori."

Rae's grip was firm and confident, that of a woman used to being in control. Her body had a gym-cultivated tightness to it. The last few women Cori had dated had that naturally strong build associated with outdoor sports. The Northwest, for all the rain, hosted a disproportionately high population of bikers, hikers, and kayakers. Rae, she suspected, was strong and lean because she wanted it that way, not because her physique was the by-product of a hobby. Her muscles spoke of hard work and determined focus. Cori wondered how much massage oil it would take to coax the tension out of them.

"Cori?" Rae flipped her blond-streaked bangs out of her eyes and released Cori from the prolonged handshake. "Nice name."

Cori snapped to attention when Rae's palm touched her thigh. Eyes, deep and blue like the ocean, focused on Cori's face as Rae traced casual circles over her skin.

"How long are you going to be in Vegas, Cori?"

It was a simple question. One that Cori wanted to answer. First, she needed to remember what day it was. Then she'd be able to figure out how many days she had left. The task proved impossible. Finally, she went with a vague but honest response. "A few days."

"Well," Rae gave her leg a final pat and stood, "I look forward to seeing you again."

Before Cori could engage her brain and offer a suitable reply, Rae walked back the way she came and disappeared into the dark casino.

"Hot damn," Julie whispered.

"Indeed."

Cori sucked on her drink, more to keep herself from chasing Rae across the patio and pinning her against the wall, than out of actual thirst. Her first chance to get a little wild in Vegas, and possibly a little horizontal, and she'd blown it. She decided that if she saw Rae again, she wouldn't hold herself back.

❖

The No Smoking placard in the break room taunted Rae, tempting her to pull a cigarette out of her half-empty pack and set a flame to it. She forced herself to concentrate on the textbook laid open on the table. Advanced organizational behavior, a topic that generally captured her attention, failed to enrapture her as she fought her desire for nicotine. She had fifteen precious minutes to study before she needed to change and clock in for work. Damn it all to hell if a little thing like a craving would come between her and the successful completion of her classes this quarter, the crucial final quarter between her and a BA in business management. The minutes wound down, ending at the same point as her willpower, and she stuffed her books in her locker, shrugged on her uniform, and headed toward the gaming floor with a Camel dangling from her mouth.

As soon as her feet hit the red carpet, indicating it was safe to light up, she did so and power-smoked her way to the pit boss. She spotted the sexy-if-tongue-tied Latina from the pool playing blackjack, and paused to watch. A face card landed and the dealer paused, but the woman didn't increase her bet. Rae dropped her cigarette in the nearest ashtray and laid one hand on the woman's lower back. It was a light touch, intended to signal that she was there and reference their earlier encounter.

She tapped the stack of chips and leaned in close enough to be discreet. "You should double down."

The woman—was her name Cori?—gave a short laugh filled with nervous energy. "I have no idea what that means."

"You have the queen of hearts." Rae smiled and drew a heart on Cori's back with her index finger. "That's always a lucky card. And the dealer has a seven. Odds are in your favor on this hand and the rules allow you to double your bet."

The explanation about when to double down and, more importantly, when not to, was far more complex, but Rae didn't have time for a drawn-out lesson. She needed to get to work. Besides, the jackpot she was looking for was more than just a few chips on a low-stakes table.

"But if I double my bet, I double the amount I can lose, right?"

"Sure." Rae flattened her palm against Cori's back, wanting to burn her impression through the thin fabric of the shirt into the skin beneath. "But it also doubles the amount you can win. And this is Vegas. There's no payoff without a little risk." She held up a two-dollar chip and cocked her head. "What do you say, are you in?"

Cori didn't answer for several seconds, her eyes focused on Rae's lips. Finally, she blinked and said, "I'm definitely in."

"Good." Rae set the chip down in front of Cori's card and nodded to the dealer. She slipped away with a slight wink, not bothering to wait and see how the next card fell.

"What the hell was that?" Greg, the pit boss on duty, growled at her a moment later when she joined the rest of the swing-shift crew.

"A lesson on how to double down." Rae stood at easy attention, her hands clasped together behind her back, feet slightly apart. "Strictly casino business, boss."

Her friend Marco nudged her with his shoulder. "The one time I tried to give a lesson like that, the lady slapped me so hard it took a week for the handprint to fade."

"Must have been a bitch to explain to your wife."

"Are you kidding?" Marco joked. "It was my wife."

Rae nudged him back. Marco had a good life. A wife who loved him, two kids with another on the way, and the confidence of knowing he would do right by them. Rae envied him.

Greg cleared his throat and she dutifully shut up as he launched into their table assignments for the evening. Normally Rae worked tables with at least a twenty-dollar buy-in, more often fifty. Tonight Greg assigned her to table thirteen, her punishment for being disruptive and getting hotter dates than he could.

"Thirteen, are you kidding me?"

She'd protested because it was expected, but her heart wasn't in it. Greg was just doing his job, using the tools available to keep the dealers in line. Table thirteen was double cursed, first with the unlucky number most gamblers avoided, *and* it had a two-dollar buy-in. The only people who ended up betting there were generally too drunk to notice the table number or too broke to go for something bigger, or both. Most of the time, the pit boss left it closed, a testament to the profound power of superstition in the world of gamblers.

"Greg," Marco's voice held serious intent, "that seems a little harsh. She was only a few seconds behind the rest of us."

Rae appreciated his defense but stepped in before Greg ended up moving Marco to that table instead. He had a family to support and his tips made the difference between survival and financial ruin.

"It's fine, Greg," she said and headed to the table before either of them could say anything further.

It was a slow night, as she'd expected. Most gave her a wide birth, eyeing the table number with suspicion, then shuffling on. Rather than being the punishment Greg intended, the work assignment proved to be a welcome break. She was able to spend a good portion of her shift watching the good-looking Latina.

Cori moved with the fluid, natural grace of a woman aware of her body, her muscles. Yet when she noticed Rae's attention, the sensuality leaked out of her and her body stiffened with awkward tension. Rae desperately wanted to ease her anxiety, to help her relax until her clothes came off. She normally favored tall and blond, and this woman was neither. She was around five-three and her hair flowed down her back like black satin. Rather than the sporty, muscled body she craved, both in herself and others, Cori's was all curves. Big breasts, full hips, and just the right amount of hourglass at the waist. Rae imagined her hands settled on the swell of Cori's hips, pulling her close as her lips closed around a straining nipple.

"Hi, Rae." Cori slid into the tall seat opposite her. She smiled almost shyly, with a hint of I-dare-you in her eyes.

"Ready for another lesson?" Rae asked.

Cori's lips parted slightly. "I'm ready…for whatever lesson you're ready to give." She placed a chip carefully on the table and regarded Rae like she knew something Rae didn't. "My name is Cori, by the way."

"I remember." Rae's heart skipped. She hadn't expected to remember the name. Apparently Cori had made the same assumption, since she'd felt the need to remind her.

She shuffled her cards slowly, letting her desire feather out on their glossy surfaces. She normally let the machine do this part of the job, but tonight, for Cori, she wanted to drag out the experience. Also, the succinct precision of the shuffler was too cold, too impersonal for the heat flowing between them. She flipped a card in front of Cori, then another for herself, this one face down. She didn't look at it, focusing her attention on Cori.

"Six of diamonds is a tough card. The best you can hope for is soft seventeen." Rae kept her voice low and intimate.

"Soft?" Cori leaned in closer, her eyes focused on Rae's lips.

"If your second card is an ace, you'll have seven or seventeen, depending on how you play it."

"What if I get a ten?"

"That would be a hard sixteen." Rae pushed the word "hard" out with a little extra force, imagining a future demonstration of the exact differences between soft and hard. She dealt them each another card, both face up this time. "Dealer draws an ace."

Cori's second card was an eight. She scooped them up neatly and flipped them over. "At least I know when to fold."

"I hope you're not ready to call it a night yet."

"Not even close. Tell me why you're dealing both of my cards up."

"I can't show you what to do if I can't see what you have." Rae swept her eyes over Cori's body, pausing to watch the rise and fall of her chest. Then she returned her gaze to Cori's face. "Can I?"

Cori held Rae's probing stare. "No, no you can't."

Rae wanted to pull her through the nearest door and drop to her knees. Hell, if she wasn't careful, she'd forget the need for privacy and spread her out like a banquet on lucky table thirteen. But Greg was watching her too closely tonight, and Cori was the kind of woman who deserved a little more work.

"I'm off in a couple of hours." Rae strangled the voice of caution warning her not to make a real date with a tourist. "Want to go to the club with me?"

CHAPTER THREE

Music pulsed through Rae's chest and settled in her bones. She tightened her grip on Cori's hand and guided her deeper into the dark club. The DJ waved from his booth and raised his brow, his head inclined toward Cori. The implied question had already followed her through the room, reflected in the eyes of every employee they'd encountered. Rae always entered a scene alone and left with a playmate, not the other way around. Starting the evening with Cori at her side was unexpected to say the least.

She merely smiled at the DJ as she led Cori toward a door near the stage. "Want to meet the band before they go on?"

"Really?" Cori's face opened up, excited and eager.

"Absolutely." Rae stuck her head in the backstage door and called out. She didn't want to catch anyone in a potentially embarrassing situation so she waited for a response before saying, "Come on."

Backstage was nothing more than an oversized dressing room filled with costumes and smoke. The lead singer, Nikki, sat in front of a mirror, carefully applying makeup. The bass player straddled an unknown woman on the couch, grinding her hips in slow, tight circles. The drummer, Kel, invited Rae over to the corner where she sat tapping out a rhythm on a five-gallon bucket. The staccato beat was unpolished and brash, blending perfectly with the music spilling out of the club speakers.

The lead guitar player emerged from the bathroom, tugging the rhythm guitar player along after her. They both wore dazed, freshly fucked smiles. Rae had limited her contact with the two of them after an ill-fated pickup attempt on the shaggy blond lead guitarist ended with her longtime lover in Rae's face with violent intentions. Determined to ignore the couple, she sank down in a stuffed armchair, settled Cori on her lap, and made the necessary introductions.

Kel's lips curved into a predatory smile. "Nice to meet you, Cori."

Cori squirmed under the scrutiny and didn't offer a handshake. Rae bristled. She knew she shouldn't be surprised by Kel's reaction. Cori was smoking hot and obviously not Rae's type. The logical conclusion was that Rae had brought her backstage to share. It wouldn't have been the first time.

"She's with me." Rae tried to keep the growl out of her voice but the words sounded overly protective to her ears. She didn't know who was more surprised, she or Kel.

Cori relaxed, her body pressing intimately close in the dark. "It's nice to meet you, Kel."

Kel nodded, dim surprise in her eyes. Her demeanor instantly changed from woman-on-the-prowl to friendly.

"So, what's up?" Rae asked her.

"The usual. What are you two doing after the show?"

What indeed? Rae shrugged.

"Come back to my place. We're having a going-away party for Nikki."

Rae pressed her lips to Cori's ear and kept her voice low. "Nikki's the lead singer, the one in front of the mirror. She's moving to L.A." To Kel she said, "When's her last show?"

"Friday."

"Gonna miss you, Nik," Rae called to the singer.

"Aw, thanks, sweetie. I'm going to miss you, too."

Strains of "Closer" by Nine Inch Nails halted all conversation. Kel stood and tapped the bucket with her sticks one last time. "They're playing our song."

Rae urged Cori off her lap. "Time to go."

They headed back to the dance floor as the band members prepared to take the stage.

Rae leaned in close to be heard over the drowning bass thump. "Ready for a drink?"

She could feel Cori's breath. The sensation tingled all the way to her toes. Rae got lost in the feeling, welcoming it, holding it close. Normally, she didn't respond physically until the moment right before climax, and she was used to being the one who caused reactions. Her body was muted to the charms of strange women in the dark, but Cori's effect left her off balance and wanting more.

Cori's laughter sounded uneasy. "I'm not sure I should drink around you."

Rae met her gaze and held it. "Then dance with me?"

Cori nodded and they fought their way to the middle of the throng of surging, sweaty bodies. Rae turned Cori so they were back to front, her hands low on Cori's hips. Guiding her in a seductive rhythm, she snuggled Cori tight against her. The club wasn't Saturday-night crowded but it was still packed, barely leaving room to breathe. Cori pressed back, her ass tight and suggestive against Rae.

She angled her head, bringing her cheek flush with Rae's. "You're the right kind of dangerous."

The words were barely a whisper, lost against Rae's skin, and she wasn't even sure if she'd heard or imagined them. She trailed her lips along Cori's neck, moaning at the sweet, citrus scent mingled with the sharp taste of sweat-salty skin. She nipped at Cori's ear, catching the lobe between her teeth and biting gently.

"I'm not dangerous at all. Not to you."

Rae didn't understand why she was willing to give Cori more than a few stolen moments, but she was. Hell, she knew nothing about her other than that she was new to blackjack and didn't live in Vegas. Just looking at her made Rae's heart pound like a damn kettledrum, and her knees turned to Jell-O with her touch.

Cori turned in her arms until they were face-to-face, their lips kissing-close. Rae ran her tongue over her bottom lip, completely transfixed by the dark invitation in Cori's eyes. She dipped her head and kissed Cori lightly, just a brush to ask permission. Cori moaned against her and the silky-smooth press of her lips gave way to an insistent need, a bold touch.

Rae parted her lips to invite Cori in. Her head swam with the power in Cori's tongue. Stroking against her. Invading her mouth. Owning her. She retreated, dizzy with want.

Cori's breath was hot against her ear, her voice low and sexy. "Let's get out of here."

Rae collected herself, caging the storming need inside her, and led her out of the club.

For a long, blinding moment, Cori couldn't breathe, couldn't think as Rae pushed her against the wall, muscles coiled tight, pinning her in place. She could only react, her skin aching from the contact. She marveled at the change in Rae. In the elevator, walking down the long corridor to Cori's room, Rae had been sweet, almost shy. The endearing hesitation disappeared when the electronic lock on the door beeped and granted them entrance.

Now she was pure fire, heat pouring off her in waves, searing Cori with its intensity. She let her head fall back, opening the curve of her neck to Rae's hot assault. She felt the flick of Rae's tongue in the sweet spot where neck melts into shoulder, a gentle, curious lick, followed instantly by a low growl and the sharp edge of teeth. She felt the bite explode in the pit of her stomach and arched her body, begging for more.

"God, you're…" Rae pulled back, her blue eyes dark and probing. "Perfect."

Cori had been holding her breath, waiting for Rae's judgment, and when it came, she melted and stretched, like a flower reaching for the sun. This wasn't smart, falling into bed with a woman she'd just met, a woman who made her weak with desire, bringing her need for release screaming to the surface with a look and the slightest touch. Was it always like this in Vegas? Overwhelming, almost frantic? She didn't care. All she wanted was for Rae to reach inside her, to know her.

She gripped the edge of Rae's shirt, a tight black tank that would look really good on the hotel room floor. Rae lowered the zipper on the back of Cori's dress and pulled it off her shoulders, exposing her skin and leaving her top half almost naked and vulnerable in the neon light coming in through the window. Then, with an impatient tug, Rae's tank was off and her body pressed against Cori's.

Cori was flooded with white-hot desire as their skin touched. "So good," she groaned, desperate for more.

Rae's hands were everywhere at once, smoothing over her waist, scratching down her sides, fisted in her hair, tracing the line of her jaw, pushing insistently at her dress until it fell to the floor. Cori focused on the touch, her world reduced to the bowstring-tight response of her body. And then there was nothing but stark cold. She fought for control, her breath coming in heaving gasps as Rae pulled further away from her. She whimpered at the loss, then felt a gentle pressure on her hand. Rae's fingers twined with hers, squeezing hard, guiding her away from the wall toward the first of two queen beds.

"Not that one, it's Julie's. My friend, remember?"

God, what if Julie came back to the room? Would they be able to stop? Or would she invite Julie to pull up a chair and watch?

Rae switched directions, leading her to the bed closest to the window. She didn't release Cori's hand as she drew back the blankets and eased Cori down on her back. She stared at her, evaluating, assessing, her need obvious, simmering just below the surface.

"I could get lost in you."

Cori watched the words form, touched by Rae's brave vulnerability. She waited, laid out for Rae's inspection, for her pleasure, not wanting to rush but barely able to hold back. And when Rae finally, slowly lowered her mouth to Cori's, all the lights in Vegas exploded behind her eyelids and shot through her body. The kiss was exquisitely gentle and undemanding. Cori opened herself, letting Rae explore with her tongue. The whisper-soft touch grew into a pounding pulse and Cori couldn't hold back. She gripped Rae's body, overwhelmed by the thrill of the warm weight holding her down.

She slid her hands lower, frustrated when she realized Rae hadn't removed her jeans. "Off." She tugged at the belt loops. "These come off now."

She wiggled her fingers around to the front. Button fly. She released one button and licked the sweat from Rae's neck. Another button and she arched, pressing her thigh hard against Rae's center. Another and she sucked and nipped Rae's pulse point, excited to hear her breath catch and feel her heart pound harder.

Rae jumped up and tore her jeans and underwear off, searing Cori with a gut-burning look. She brushed her hands up Cori's legs and slid her fingers beneath the lace edge of her panties. She lowered them in slow degrees. Cori writhed, pressing her ass against the bed, anything for a little relief from the building pressure between her thighs.

The hard, lean lines of Rae's muscles were bathed in light from the street below. The sight made Cori's hands itch with desire to touch, to penetrate. She sat up and removed her bra, not wanting to wait any longer for Rae to finish undressing her. A bolt of liquid fire gripped her low in her belly as Rae stared hungrily at her breasts. Cori cupped them, teasing the nipples, daring Rae to return to the bed, to claim what was offered.

Rae gasped, muscles clenched, chest heaving. She stepped away, shoulders to the wall, and swayed against it, her eyes riveted on Cori's hands, her breasts.

"You like this?" Cori squeezed harder.

"Yes." It was a ragged gasp, barely audible.

Cori slid one hand lower, caressing her belly, daring Rae, taunting her. She paused just below her navel, her hand flat, her fingers spread over her abdomen. This wasn't exactly what she'd planned when she invited Rae up to her room. She'd imagined a hot, fast fuck. But watching Rae hold herself back, panting with desire, burned into her, penetrating far deeper than a touch. Cori spread her legs, shivering as the cool air touched her wet sex.

"I want you, Rae." She fingered her clit, sliding over the impossibly slick folds and dipping just inside. "Do you see how much?"

Rae stared at her, eyes wide, her hands limp at her sides. "Yes."

Cori carved a glistening trail back up her body with the wet finger, circling first one, then the other nipple. Rae's eyes followed. Cori brought her hand to her mouth, painting her lips before sucking her finger in. Rae's self-control amazed her and she longed to break it. "Do you want a taste?"

"God, yes." Rae didn't move.

Frustration shook Cori, making her throb with need. She spread her legs wider. If this was the way Rae wanted her, trembling and ready to come under her own touch, then she would give it to her. She moved her hand back to her aching center, the teasing foreplay gone. No more shy exploration. She went straight for her clit with intense, practiced motions, circling, stroking, feeling herself grow pebble hard. She arched and strained, so close she could feel the beginning tremors gathering in her belly. Her legs shook and she wanted to close her eyes and give herself over to the moment, but she couldn't. Rae's glazed stare was filled with lust and longing, pushing Cori higher. She searched Rae's face for permission, a sign that she wanted her to take herself over the edge.

With a keening moan, Rae stumbled closer and dropped to her knees on the bed, her breath hot against Cori's thighs. Still she didn't touch her.

"I'm going to come. Please, Rae."

"Yesss." Rae dove into her, stretching her, filling her with molten heat. She withdrew and crawled up Cori's body, punctuating her progress with another deep, hard thrust.

Cori's body exploded, coming apart and floating back together in a blinding white light as Rae reached her goal, invading her mouth, fucking her with her tongue and fingers. Relentless. Hard. Cori felt Rae shudder against her, groaning and twisting before collapsing in a boneless heap on top of her. Gathering Rae to her, she feathered kisses over her hair, her eyes, her ears, everywhere she could reach.

"That was…" She let the sentence die, unsure how to finish it, how to explain everything that happened inside her, the beauty that led up to the orgasm and the peace that followed.

"Yes, it most certainly was." Rae breathed into Cori's neck, sending tremors down her body. She rolled over with Cori in her arms, cradling her, making her feel safe.

Cori exhaled and snuggled close, burying her face in Rae's shoulder, breathing her in. She'd expected Rae to run before the languid afterglow settled over them. Instead, Cori felt warm and protected, enough to last through the night. The familiarity of their embrace left unanswered questions in her mind, questions she wasn't prepared to think about. This was enough, for now. She'd worry about what it all meant tomorrow.

Chapter Four

L ight streamed through the window. Daylight, not the manufactured neon that kept the city perpetually awake. Rae squeezed her eyes shut, the bright assault on her pupils adding to the pounding timpani behind her temples. She rolled over and moaned, trying to determine her location without looking. The too-firm mattress told her it was a hotel room. She searched her fuzzy mind for the reason she was here instead of sleeping in her own apartment.

A hand settled on her waist, the fingers smoothing over her skin in light, rhythmic circles. She cracked open her eyes. Cori's sleepy smile filled her with warmth, and the pain in her head receded to a dull pressure. She covered Cori's hand with her own and held it flat against her stomach, stilling the movement. Then she brought the fingers to her mouth and kissed them gently.

"Hi." Cori brushed her fingers over Rae's face. The touch was light yet searching, like Cori was trying to memorize every detail.

The intense focus in her eyes made Rae's body hum. She wanted to pounce on her, hungry and fast, but she closed her eyes and held herself still, surrendering to the moment and allowing Cori enough privacy to learn what she needed.

They stayed like that for several long moments, stretched out side by side, not touching beyond Cori's gentle exploration. Rae waited for her internal alarms to wake up, to scream that it was time to go, but the usual compulsion to leave never happened. Just like the night before, when she would normally walk out the door, she simply shifted closer and held Cori tight against her.

This was uncharted territory. Rae didn't *do* the morning after and had only a vague idea what was expected of her. She'd heard horror stories from friends who were either too drunk or too stupid to leave before morning. Hell, she even had some faded memories of her own, experiences that had taught her to get dressed and escape before the afterglow faded. Still, she had a feeling Cori's expectations were different from most. Her touch lacked the clinging desperation of buyer's remorse. Rae didn't feel pressured. Cori seemed to want nothing beyond the moment.

The unmistakable sound of the door being unlocked interrupted Rae's introspection. She grabbed the edge of the blanket from below her hips and dragged it up. "Roommate?"

"Afraid so." The contentment drained from Cori's face and was replaced with careful indifference.

The woman who'd been with Cori by the pool yesterday tiptoed into the room, her strappy sandals dangling from one hand. They fell to the floor with a thunk-thunk. "Sorry." Her startled gaze landed on Cori. "I didn't realize you had company."

Rae offered a devil-may-care smile. "And that's my cue to leave."

Her attempt to throw back the blanket was aborted when Cori held it firmly in place. She lowered her lashes. "You're naked."

Rae smiled. She couldn't help it. Last night Cori had been wanton and uninhibited. Her sudden shyness and modesty were unexpected, to say the least.

The roommate shifted uncertainly from one foot to the other before moving toward the bathroom. "I'll just be in here."

The door clicked shut behind her giving them a few minutes of privacy. Rae plucked at the edge of the comforter, not ready for her time with Cori to end. While she was thinking about how nice it had been to just lie with her, Cori leaned over and kissed her. Not a hard, demanding kiss like those that had driven Rae crazy the night before, but a gentle, sweet, and lingering press of lips. Rae luxuriated in the light caress, enjoying the tenderness of it, letting it fill her up.

When the kiss ended, she rested her forehead against Cori's. "I really do need to go."

"I know." Cori's dark eyes were sad but resolved.

Rae slipped out of bed and dressed, her gaze never leaving Cori. She swallowed a request for them to see each other again. She rarely went back for seconds, and on those infrequent occasions the liaison was simply a matter of circumstance. Sometimes she ran into a woman more than once, but she *never* sought out additional contact. Now, without her usual indifference, her cool style crumbled into awkward silence. She offered Cori a careful smile and made her way to the door.

"Rae?"

"Yes?" Did she really sound as eager as she thought?

"It was good to be with you."

Rae merely nodded, lost for words and disoriented by an urge to rush to the bed and kiss Cori again. Shaking off the unfamiliar feeling, she produced a sexy grin and escaped into the hall. Despite the cautionary voice in the back of her head, she moved easily down the thick carpet toward the elevators, the spring of hope in her steps. It wouldn't be wise, she knew, to see Cori again, but she looked forward to the next time she spied her at the blackjack tables.

❖

"Cori, do you think we should actually attend any of the seminars?"

Julie didn't sound the slightest bit sorry as she sipped her drink. Who could blame her? Sunlight glinted off the pool, a taunting reminder that they weren't in Seattle and this rare time out was precious. Days like this shouldn't be spent in stuffy conference rooms listening to boring lectures.

Cori shrugged. "Maybe I'll take in a session tomorrow."

"Where's your new friend when we need her?" Julie held up her empty glass as though it might magically refill itself.

Cori stared down at the ice cubes in her own glass and wondered if there was any rum residue she could lick from them. Did she just finish number three or four? She couldn't remember, but another one seemed in order. She smiled weakly at the memory of Rae's hand on her thigh as she casually introduced herself the first day.

"I doubt we'll see her today."

"Really? She seemed kind of into you this morning."

That was true. Rae *had* been into her that morning. Then she'd walked out the door without a backward glance. "I got the impression that two dates constitutes a long-term relationship for her."

"You guys went on a date? I thought you just fucked."

The poolside server arrived with a fresh drink for each of them. God bless Vegas. It was the only place in the world you could get a judgment-impairing, bright blue, frozen rum drink refilled poolside at one in the afternoon.

"I definitely got fucked." Cori considered Julie's statement beyond just the teasing poke she'd intended. "But before that we went to a club and danced. She even introduced me to the band. Pretty sure it was a date. If it wasn't, I need to reevaluate the way I say good night."

"You realize I'm totally jealous?" Julie didn't sound jealous at all. "She's unreasonably hot."

"Yes." Cori needed to change the subject. Dwelling on what was sure to be a one-time-only event would only make her want to see Rae even more. And since she wasn't likely to get another date, there was no point in thinking about it. "What about you? You were out all night."

"Believe it or not, I ran into a woman from high school. She lives here now."

"Small world." Cori took a long pull on her drink. The buzz settled in her stomach and radiated outward. God only knew where her feet were because she couldn't feel them anymore. All in all, it was a perfect way to spend the day, lying in the sun next to the pool with an endless supply of drinks. She was glad Julie was in Las Vegas to share the manufactured oasis with her.

"She told me about a party tonight," Julie continued. "I said we'd go."

"Sure, why not?" Cori could think of at least one reason not to go. Rae. If there was a chance to spend more time with her, she wanted to take it, and vanishing for the evening would do little for her prospects. She could go to parties in Seattle.

Staring into her drink, she resolved to wait and see and what happened. Julie would understand if a better offer came up. They relaxed into an easy sun-baked quiet Cori hoped would continue. She needed the rest.

"Tell me more about your night," Julie asked after a few moments. "You said you got to meet the band. That sounds cool."

Cori tried to call the experience to mind. She'd been so captivated by Rae that the details about the women in the band were fuzzy. The room had been filled with smoke, the smell of sex, and the constant pounding of drumsticks on a five-gallon bucket. If she squeezed her mind hard enough, surely she could pick out a fact interesting enough to share.

"The lead singer is leaving," she said. "Tomorrow night is her last show here."

"That explains all the signs."

"Signs?"

Since Julie was a would-be astrologer, Cori didn't know if the signs she was referring to were ethereal or literal.

"Flyers. All over the place. They're having open auditions today."

"I hadn't noticed." And that was the kind of thing that would normally grab Cori's attention. There was still enough of the little girl singing into a hairbrush inside of her to keep her rock star fantasy alive and well. Even though she didn't give the fantasy any credibility, she would usually have paid some attention to a flyer announcing auditions.

"You should try out."

Cori snorted, barely able to keep blue ice from shooting out her nose.

"Seriously, you should," Julie persisted. "I've heard you sing."

"No, you've heard me karaoke. There's a big difference." Belting out eighties glam metal to a room full of people too drunk to realize when she was half a step too high was one thing. A working band in Vegas was quite another.

"What about Mari's wedding? You sounded great then."

"I forgot you were there."

Maricel, the oldest of Cori's five siblings, was the same age as Julie. They were pretty good friends in school, but when Mari said "I do" she left behind her single life, including her friends, in favor of domestic bliss. Cori didn't believe Mari had shunned her old friends intentionally. Omitting them from social events was just a natural separation born from not sharing common lifestyles. A few years later, Julie and Cori had both ended up at Eden Body Works and naturally gravitated to one another.

Singing during her sister's wedding had been a big risk for Cori. It was her first public appearance, outside of her high school choir, and she'd insisted on positioning herself behind a screen, out of her father's direct line of sight. At the time, he'd been angling for a promotion and wanted a string quartet to impress his boss, who loved classical music. For once Cori's sister hadn't bent to his overwhelming will. She'd asked Cori to sing and it had taken several hastily consumed glasses of rum to loosen her vocal cords that day.

"That wedding was straight out of a fairytale." Julie sighed. "When she walked down the aisle, I've never seen her happier." There was a trace of sadness in her voice.

"Yeah, she really loves him."

Even though Cori didn't want to find a husband, a part of her was envious of her sister. Mari's husband was singular in his devotion. The sun rose and set at Mari's feet, as far as he was concerned. Cori wouldn't mind finding someone like that to share her life with.

"And that song, what was it?" Julie's face wore a thoughtful expression. "'Grow Old With Me'?"

"Yes." Their parents had fought against the classic John

Lennon song for the processional, wanting a more traditional wedding march, but when the moment came the choice was perfect.

"Beautiful." Julie heaved a sigh.

Refusing to join her on another sentimental contemplation of true love and all they were missing out on, Cori cast a searching look around the pool area for the hundredth time and took another long sip of her drink. She felt foolish, but she couldn't keep herself from looking for Rae. Talk about her sister's real-life happy ending made her crave Rae's company even more. Rather than think about what that might mean, she struggled out of her lounger. "I'm getting another drink."

"Oh, no you don't." Julie leapt up with the grace of a sober ballerina and latched on to Cori's arm. "You've got an audition to go to. Let's go."

The sight of Rae inside the casino, dressed in her work uniform and striding purposefully toward the tables, stopped Cori's protest before it could solidify. Her mouth was instantly cotton-dry as she followed Julie through the crush of people and felt-covered tables. Ahead of them, Rae moved with precision and strength. Her body showed none of the tension and confusion Cori was struggling with. Cori's mind raced through a thousand reasons to just walk up to her. No matter what excuse she fabricated, the scenario ended one of two ways in her head: With them naked, rolling around on the floor, gamblers be damned. Or with Rae blinking at her in confusion, their encounter forgotten in the bright light of day.

Both options would bring her to her knees, and she wasn't prepared for either outcome. She let Julie drag her along, not quite registering where they were going until they stopped outside the club entrance.

"You here to audition?" asked a blonde whose outfit

and demeanor said she was trying for rock chic but had only achieved rock wannabe.

"She is." Julie pushed Cori forward before she could object.

"Okay, here's your number." The wannabe exposed an adhesive strip and started to affix a slip of paper to Cori's midsection. She stopped short when she realized she was dealing with bare flesh. Cori was wearing a two-piece bathing suit. "Uh, where do you want it?"

"I'll take it," Julie said.

"Right." The blonde looked confused, like this slight break in her routine set her impossibly off track. "So, fill this out." She held up a form, wavering between Cori and Julie, and after a slight pause, handed it to Julie, also. "And here's the song list. Pick out a few you're comfortable with and return everything to me when you're done."

Julie tugged Cori deeper into the club. "You fill this out. I'm going to get you something to wear. Be right back." She shoved the papers into Cori's hands.

"This isn't a good idea," Cori said.

"Why not? At the very least, you sing better than her." Julie gestured toward the woman currently on the stage mutilating an old Elton John song.

Cori winced. "I'm not sure that qualifies as singing."

"Pick out your songs, and I'll be right back." Julie finished the sentence over her shoulder as she walked away. That was how she ended most disagreements. She simply went forward with her plans without giving the other person a chance to interject.

Cori hesitated, wondering if she could do this. Why not? They were here and Julie wasn't going to leave her alone until she sang something. Cori completed the paperwork, made her song selections, and turned everything in. Then she settled against the bar and waited for someone to call her number.

CHAPTER FIVE

Rae lit her cigarette as she stepped through the door to the club. She only had a few minutes until the end of her lunch break, but she wanted to check on the auditions and see how her friends were doing with their search for a new singer.

"Hey, El, find anyone yet?" she asked the band's manager.

Ellen nodded toward the stage. "She's pretty good."

Rae was surprised to see Cori under the spotlight listening closely to what Kel was saying from behind her drums. "Really?"

"Yeah. They've dismissed most everybody after a verse or two, but they've kept her up there for a while."

The house lights were up, so the spotlight wouldn't obscure the rest of the room from view, but Rae doubted Cori would be able to see her. She leaned against the wall, next to Ellen, and just watched.

Cori wrapped her hands around the mic, loose and easy. Rather than waiting for Kel to count the song in, she sang the refrain of Nina Simone's "Since I Fell for You" a cappella. Her voice resonated through Rae like the soothing burn of good whiskey and brought the hair on her arms and neck to attention. After two full beats of silence, Kel crashed in on the drums, dragging the guitarists along for the hard, driving ride. The band forced the silky-smooth soul song up tempo and added a bastardized punk brashness.

Cori stayed with them, her dark, textured voice pulsing from sorrow to rage. Her harsh passion left Rae breathless and unable to think beyond a throbbing need for more. When the song ended, the room felt like a vacuum, all the sound sucked from the air. Rae's heart raced, beating against her chest. A wild, heady need for Cori coursed through her body.

Noises began to filter back into the room, the clink of glasses at the bar, the low murmur of other hopefuls waiting to audition, the steady scratch of Ellen's pen on paper. Rae clutched at the smooth surface of the wall, trying to catch her breath. She looked around, wondering if Cori had had the same effect on everyone, or just on her. The others appeared to have enjoyed the song, but no one seemed as wrung by it as she was. She glanced over Ellen's shoulder. The notes she'd written about the performance were complimentary, but nothing there indicated that the experience was soul shattering.

Somehow Cori's voice brought Rae to her knees and left her wanting more. Images flooded her mind. Cori, legs spread, teasing her clit to hard attention. Rae wanted to hear her moan—no, scream—through her orgasm with the same pounding emotion she'd poured into the song. She couldn't shake the urge to approach Cori and touch her. With a shock of dismay, she watched Cori move closer to Kel as they talked about the performance. Here she was, auditioning for the band. Did that mean she was entertaining the thought of staying in Vegas, of stepping into Rae's world instead of kissing her good-bye? That would change everything.

Rae needed to sit down. Her flings didn't *stay*. They left with kisses as sweet as they were mercifully final. *Good-bye, have a nice life* was the message, not *Hello, which side of the closet is mine?* Stumbling to the nearest chair, Rae tried to remember where Cori was from. Had she even asked? Probably not, and maybe she wasn't serious about the audition, anyway. Maybe people had told her she could sing, and she wanted to find out for sure. She would leave, happy with the endorsement.

Rae wished she could hear what Kel was saying. She didn't need a degree in rocket science to read the intensity in each woman's expression. Kel might not be offering her the gig, but she was giving her reason to think she had a good chance, that much was obvious from the thrilled disbelief on Cori's face. Rae could hardly believe it. She made a conscious effort to step back from her feelings and take a positive view.

Cori was talented, and deserved the offer. Adding her would change the look and appeal of the band. Nikki was a Nordic goddess, tall and big-boned, with blond hair, fake tan, and blue eyes that penetrated across a smoke-filled bar. Cori was all curves, her eyes so dark and tempting you could fall into them and never find a way out. Nikki was new Vegas flash and Cori was old Vegas torch. She was the real thing, pure neon inspiration, and perfect. Rae wanted to feast on her for days.

Days, she repeated mentally.

While Cori remained in the realm of unfulfilled possibility, Rae was in familiar territory. But if she moved to Vegas, all bets were off. Cori would be potential relationship material. Rae gave her a long look. Why the sudden urge to relocate? Her pulse raced. Perspiration rose around her hairline. Surely Cori wasn't one of those women who thought one hot night meant marriage.

She took one last shaky drag on her Camel and crushed it out. "I have to get back to work," she told Ellen.

She would look for Cori later and casually ask how the

audition went. If she was lucky, Cori might even give her a private concert in her room. And if the topic of her move to Vegas came up, Rae would play it cool. She could hear herself: *Sure, why not. Hey, you and I could even hook up again sometime…*

❖

Cori left the audition feeling wrung out. She hadn't worked that hard at singing since she graduated and left her high school choir behind, along with her crush on the teacher.

Julie bounced with enthusiasm. "Oh, wow. I'll have a place to stay the next time I come to Vegas."

"Not so fast," Cori said. "I'm not moving."

There was no way she was going to leave Seattle and move to the desert. The whole notion was absurd. Her family, her career, hell, her *life* was in Washington. She couldn't just pack up and leave everything behind. Could she? Besides, Kel had given her some flattering compliments, but she hadn't offered her the spot.

"Why not?" Julie asked. "What's to stop you?"

"I'm not having this conversation." The effect of the drinks she'd enjoyed earlier by the pool had faded, leaving her sober and a little irritated that she'd wasted the afternoon chasing an impossible dream. She spotted Rae working one of the tables and started in that direction. Rae would probably tell her to get lost, but Cori couldn't stop herself. She wanted to see her again.

"I'm going to say hi to Rae." She smiled at Julie to soften her next sentence. "I'll catch up with you later, okay?"

"You're ditching me?"

Both hands on her hips, Julie looked like a little kid about to stomp her foot. But her whining dropped out of focus, becoming nothing more than loud background noise, when Rae looked up and met Cori's gaze. Cori gave her a finger wave, the kind obnoxious straight girls gave their boyfriends when they were trying to be demure. She immediately wished she could take it back. Maybe the alcohol hadn't worn off completely, after all.

She slipped into an empty seat at Rae's table. "Hi."

"You going to play a hand?"

Cori glanced at the placard on the front of the table. Fifty-dollar buy-in. "No." She stood hastily. "I just wanted to say hi."

"I'm on my break in a few minutes. Hang around for a bit?"

Cori wanted to do celebratory back flips but settled for saying, "Yeah. I'll be over there." She motioned toward the slots.

Slot machines held little appeal for her. Put a dollar in, pull a handle. Put another dollar in, pull a handle. Hell, with the newer machines, there wasn't even a handle, just a big plastic button. In her experience, the amount of money that came out of the machine didn't come close to the amount that went in. Still, she couldn't just sit there and do nothing, so she gave it a whirl. Five dollars and about thirty seconds later, her original opinion was confirmed.

"Not nearly as much fun as blackjack, is it?" Rae whispered in her ear.

A cascade of goose bumps rolled down Cori's body. "No," she mumbled, and Rae's arms closed around her waist from behind, drawing her near.

"I have some extra time. My friend Tami is going to miss her break so she can cover. Come with me?"

"God, yes." Cori wanted to drag Rae up to her room but knew there wasn't time.

She laced her fingers into Rae's and let herself be led to a door labeled Staff Only. The dimly lit room they entered was filled with old slot machines. Not her idea of a perfect place for a romantic interlude, but it would have to do.

From behind her, Rae nuzzled her neck. "I missed you today."

Cori dropped her head to the side, inviting Rae's mouth to sizzle across the sensitive skin just below her ear. "Yeah?"

"Oh, yeah."

The night before, Cori had held herself open to Rae, vulnerable and pleading. Today she needed more, she needed to *know* her. With a growl, she stepped away from Rae and twisted in her arms. "It's my turn."

She pushed her body against Rae's, imprinting her will through the layers of clothing and the slow grind of her hips, until she felt Rae impact against the closed door with a soft thud.

"God, I want you." Cori's words died against Rae's mouth, in a tangle of tongues, lips, and the sharp edge of teeth.

Rae tightened her grip and Cori thought for a moment that she was going to hold her at bay, then she relaxed, her arms falling to her sides in surrender. "I'm yours."

For how long? Cori choked back the question, unwilling to ask for more than she would be granted. She worked her hands between them, palms flat against Rae's abdomen. She forced herself to go slow, to focus on Rae. A slight tremor stirred beneath her hands, the pulse beating fast just below Rae's jawline. Rae's breath was jagged and harsh. Cori closed her eyes and kissed her, gentle, exploring, building to a demanding crescendo as she opened Rae's slacks.

She didn't tease the skin under Rae's shirt, didn't try to gain access to the nipples straining to be licked. She sucked Rae's tongue into her mouth, glided over it, and tasted the soft mint of her gum. Breathless with longing, she slid her hand beneath Rae's panties and down past the slick, wet heat. A loud moan pushed past her lips as she eased her fingers into Rae. There was no room for the rhythmic in and out between the tight pressure of Rae's pants and the clench of her internal muscles. Cori flexed her fingers and curled them back, drawing Rae even closer.

Rae gasped, "So good."

Cori traced her tongue along Rae's ear. "That's it, right there." She worked her fingers back and forth, watching Rae twitch, her body coiled tight with need. She didn't let up, didn't press forward. She kept Rae on the edge, wanting her to beg. "Tell me what you want, Rae."

"God." She shook her head, eyes clenched tight. "I want…"

Cori quickened her pace, her arm straining against the tight space. "Tell me."

"I want…"

Cori pushed her thigh against the back of her hand, using it to increase the rocking pressure inside Rae. She felt Rae tighten, on the brink of release. "Tell me."

Rae's head rolled back, her body shook. "You." She clutched Cori, her grip bruising. "I want you."

Cori held Rae through the climax, slowing her fingers, then easing them out as Rae hung off her, limp and panting. Minutes ticked by and Rae stayed in her embrace, supple and relaxed, her head resting against Cori's shoulder. Cori could feel the muscles flexing and firming as Rae collected herself. Rae was sexy on the prowl, but Cori found this soft vulnerability much more appealing. More real.

"That was," Rae's mouth curved into a slow, sexy smile, "unexpected."

"Yes." This encounter was another line on a long list of

the unexpected during her week in Vegas, starting with her reaction to Rae.

The alarm on Rae's wristwatch sounded and she sprang into motion. "Fuck. I'm late." She fastened her pants, tucked in her shirt, and ran her fingers through her hair with practiced precision.

Cori followed her out of the room. A sick feeling rode like lead in her stomach as realization settled over her. This wasn't Rae's first trip to the storage closet, and Cori doubted it would be the last.

❖

Rae rushed through the locker room banter after her shift. As much as she enjoyed her coworkers, Cori was somewhere in the casino and Rae had to find her. She started her search at the blackjack tables. Even though she hadn't seen Cori since their encounter, she'd hoped that by the time she changed into her street clothes Cori would be here. For reasons she wasn't eager to explore, it seemed important that their time together had affected Cori as much as it had *her*. Not that she was affected on anything but a physical level, she argued internally. She didn't allow casual encounters with tourists to blossom into anything serious emotionally. It just wasn't safe. So why was she wasting time searching for a woman who would be gone in a few days?

"What are you doing tonight, Rae?" Tami asked. The redhead worked the same shift as Rae and they often went out together afterward. She helped Rae out occasionally, distracting Greg if she was running late.

Rae shrugged. "Nothing in particular."

It wasn't entirely true. She planned to track down Cori and…do what exactly? She wasn't sure. She just didn't feel like fighting her body's needs. She should have made plans with Cori that afternoon, but she wasn't thinking properly at the time. Her brain was clouded in the afterglow.

As she and Tami approached the club, a heavy techno beat poured out to greet them. A group of women crossed their path, clearly dressed up for a night out in the city of sin.

Tami watched them with exaggerated interest. "Oh, my."

One of the women—tall, blond, and looking for trouble—turned at the sound of Tami's voice. Her gaze skimmed over Tami and landed on Rae with obvious intent. She was exactly Rae's type, even if her hair color was a little too brassy to be natural.

Tami nudged Rae in the ribs. "How'd you like to get her alone?"

Rae had made the same type of crass comment a hundred times in the past, but Tami's flippancy stabbed at her. Was that all there was to her in the minds of others—a woman who had quick fucks with strangers? She certainly hadn't given her friends and coworkers a reason to expect anything more from her. She'd never stopped to think about the women she'd been with. In her mind, they didn't exist beyond the moment. Their motivations, desires, and interests meant nothing beyond orgasm. At least she could lay claim to that. Her partners always came. She made sure of it.

But what about Cori? She was more than a forgettable liaison, worth more than thirty minutes pushed against a wall. She was the type of woman who should be taken home to meet the family, who deserved promises and a lifetime plan. All things Rae couldn't give her and shouldn't even be contemplating.

The blonde whispered something to her friends, and then made her way over to Rae and Tami. She stood in front of Rae, one hip thrust out the side, her little black dress working its way up her thigh. Rae wondered if Cori had a dress like that. She'd like to see her wearing it, and peel it off her.

"Hi." The woman's voice was high and soft like a little girl's. Nothing like Cori's rich alto. "I'm Vicky."

"Rae." Rae kissed her hand. It was the right move for a practiced seduction, but it left her cold. "This is Tami."

Vicky went through the motions with Tami, but kept her attention focused on Rae. "My friends and I are here on vacation." She motioned toward the other women. "I love Vegas, don't you? We thought we'd check out the dancing here tonight, see what kind of fun we could have."

Tami was right. Normally it would be nice to spend some time three-fingers-deep in Vicky in the storage room. With Rae's tongue down her throat she wouldn't be able to continue talking. Rae wondered if her voice would still be irritating when she was moaning. She took women to that closet because she didn't have time for more, didn't *want* time for more.

The memory of Cori backing her against the door, forcing her hand into her pants stopped Rae cold. She was suddenly irrationally bothered that she'd treated Cori the same way she treated every other woman she'd been with in the past few years. What was she trying to prove? That her attraction to Cori was just as short-lived and meaningless?

Rae frowned as a realization dawned on her. She had tried to work Cori out of her system, but her attempt had obviously backfired or she wouldn't be so uninterested in the perfectly fuckable woman standing right in front of her. This obsessive need to find Cori had to end now. Rae couldn't afford such self-indulgence. It was crazy for her think constantly of a woman she had no hope of developing a relationship with. Furthermore, when did she start wanting a relationship? The thought, and the woman who provoked it, were simply too much to contemplate. She needed to forget about Cori and return to familiar ground, enjoying herself with an unfamiliar body.

Tami looked inside the club. It was too early to judge what the night would be like. "Looks kind of lame."

"A friend of ours is having a party if you're interested," Vicky said hopefully.

Rae considered her choices. No matter how much her body craved Cori, that desire would only lead to disaster. She didn't have relationships, certainly not with tourists. Vicky sucked in her bottom lip, a pouty, sexy move that did nothing for Rae's heart rate. But she cupped the blonde's cheek anyway and traced her thumb across the welcoming lips.

"I'm going wherever you are, Vicky."

The yellow cab dropped them in front of a nondescript apartment building, too run-down to be upscale but too polished to be a slum.

"You sure this is the place?" Cori wrinkled her nose.

Old high school friend or not, she wondered how well Julie knew her seminar-long playmate. Well enough for Cori to trust her advice about a party in an unknown city, at an unknown apartment in a questionable-at-best neighborhood? The air in the parking lot was stale and hard. She wanted to climb back in the cab and return to the hotel. Even if she couldn't find Rae at the casino, she could go dancing at the club.

Cori realized that she'd spent a lot of time during this trip being led forcibly to places she didn't really want to go. Deciding to make an excuse to Julie, she looked back, but the cab was already gone.

"Come on." Julie tugged her arm.

The building was set up like a traditional motel, with

an outside entrance to each apartment rather than an indoor corridor like she was used to. People were spilling out the front along with loud club music.

Julie pointed to an open door at the end. "That's the apartment."

They worked their way into the crowd, easing between bodies.

"Want a drink?" Cori's voice was lost in the pounding drum beat as they entered a long living room packed with women.

Julie yelled, "I'll get it." She headed toward the kitchen.

Cori gave in to the music and danced her way to the edge of the room, looking for a place to relax. She made it past the outer ring of people when she saw Rae's face through the crowd. She was in a corner, her attention elsewhere. Cori moved closer, wanting to get her attention, dance a little, and maybe take her back to the hotel. She stopped cold when she saw that Rae was with another woman. Who was half-naked. Rae drew the semi-clad blonde back against the wall with her, holding her tight.

Cori was riveted in place. She wanted to drag the woman off Rae by the roots of her peroxide-blond hair. At the same time she wanted to escape out the door. Instead she stood very still, feet cemented to the floor, and stared.

She focused exclusively on Rae, factoring out the blonde, who had just dropped to her knees. With her head thrown back and her eyes half-closed, Rae gripped the woman's head, knotting her fingers in her hair as she thrust into her. She was beautiful, feral, dangerous. But beneath her confidence and vibrant appeal, Cori saw something more, an almost indefinable quality. Sadness? Fear? Rae's movements seemed forced, like she was relying on muscle memory, rather than lust, to drive her forward. Yet she was obviously enjoying herself.

Cori licked her lips. In her mind, it was *her* hair Rae held. *Her* lips. *Her* tongue coaxing Rae into a raging hard storm. God, she wanted to taste her, see what she could learn in the flavor of her essence, find out where her breaking point was and push her past it with her tongue. Her fingers itched. She wanted everything, smooth skin, wet heat, everywhere, and right now. She wanted to make Rae sweat. She wanted to drive the memory of every other lover from her head. She wanted Rae to feel *her* lips every time she came, no matter who was kneeling in front of her. She wanted to possess Rae from the inside and fuck away the need for other women until all Rae was left with was Cori's image burned into her skin.

Rae jerked and shuddered, but she held the blonde's head in place, not granting her permission to stand. She opened her eyes slowly, pushed one hand through her hair, and met Cori's gaze across the room. Shock worked its way across her face, followed by a moment of panic, but she didn't lower her eyes.

They stared at one another, Cori's heart aching, until the blonde rose to her feet, obscuring Rae's face from view. Cori shook herself free of her inertia and pushed her way through the crowd. Once she was out the door, she ran hard, desperate to put distance between her and Rae, not trusting her emotions. But Rae's hazy, desire-flushed face chased her down the street and into the night. And it still flashed before her as she reached the hotel and rushed blindly to her room.

Cori couldn't wash that image away, standing under a hot shower, or block it by forcing herself to think of something else. Rae seemed to taunt her, making her angry and aroused all at once. Cori didn't know what was worse, hating her or wanting her.

Chapter Six

Rae paused at the bottom of the steps and her backpack threatened to slide off her shoulders completely. She hiked it into position and stared up at Beam Hall. Students surged past her on their way to class. All she had to do was release herself to the tide and flow with them to her room. But she couldn't.

A nagging voice in the back of her head chided her about the hurt she'd carelessly inflicted on Cori. She wanted to find her and explain herself. But Cori was a tourist. Surely Rae, like everything else in Vegas, was nothing more than an enjoyable distraction for her. Why did it matter what Cori thought of her?

Rae forced herself to resume her journey, only to pause again a few yards from her classroom door. Her future waited on the other side. Her classes were essential if she was going to have the career she wanted. But she couldn't shake free of the look of shock and betrayal on Cori's face last night.

It made no sense to be so disturbed by the memory. It wasn't like Rae was looking for a relationship. If it didn't matter, why wasn't she sitting inside her classroom right now? The stream of students around her lightened until she stood alone, no closer to seizing the future she'd mapped out for herself. Finally, she gave up resisting. She had to find Cori and make things right between them.

She arrived at the hotel after a near miss with an enthusiastic if inattentive driver behind the wheel of a rental sedan. The express elevator moved in a painful crawl. Now that she was committed to finding Cori, she couldn't get there quick enough. When she arrived at Cori's floor, doubt overwhelmed her. What would she do if Cori refused to see her? If she told her to go away? The thought sent a ripple of panic through her. She couldn't let that happen.

She dragged her leaden feet down the corridor and stopped in front of Cori's door. She didn't knock. What could she say? Could she tell Cori that she'd been with her, in her mind, the night before? That she'd felt nothing until she replaced the blonde's image with a memory of Cori. That the thought of Cori's tongue on her had sent her trembling over the edge. Worse, what if knowing that Rae had been thinking of her but had sex with a stranger anyway hurt Cori further?

With that last thought fresh in her mind, Rae turned away from the door. She couldn't face her. And when it came right down to it, an apology wouldn't matter anyway. Cori would soon be gone, leaving Rae behind to resume her life. Rae didn't believe the offer of a job with the band would make any difference. Cori had a life and a good career elsewhere. Why would she throw away her security for a gamble on a musical daydream? And, if she had any illusions about a romance, Rae had certainly dispelled those. In fact, if she tried to make up for her behavior now, she would probably be lucky to escape without getting her face slapped.

Before she could retreat to the elevator, Cori's door swung open. Rae's brain bolted, but her feet remained rooted firmly in place. She braced herself.

"Shit." Cori's friend Julie tripped backward when she saw

Rae. "You scared the crap out of me." She scrunched up her face. "You're Rae, right?"

"Yes. I need to talk to Cori."

"Cori's not here." Julie's tone revealed nothing, and her expression was locked down tight and guarded like Fort Knox. Still, Rae had to try.

"Will you tell me where she is?" She struggled to keep the tremble in her chest from reaching her voice.

"I'm not sure she wants to see you."

"No, I don't imagine she does."

Rae wanted to say more, but how could she? Lost inside the impossible swirl of her thoughts, she couldn't sort out how she could make Julie trust her. She had to convince Julie that Cori was important to her.

Julie's expression softened. "Why do you want to see her?"

Why? To tell her she was sorry. To take away the hurt in her eyes. To beg forgiveness. To just be close to her again. Rae closed her eyes. She should walk away and leave this mess behind. It would only lead to heartache.

"I don't know." It was the only real truth she could grab onto.

Julie glanced at her phone, checking the time. "She'll be in the Plateau meeting room for another fifteen minutes."

Rae blinked. She didn't know if she should shout, hug Julie, or tear off down the hall. She opted for the last choice, with a hasty thanks over her shoulder as she hustled away. The Plateau was on the other side of the property, in the convention center. She'd be able to make it in fifteen minutes if she ran and the elevator gods were on her side.

❖

Cori glanced at her watch. Only five more minutes of this half-baked hell and she'd be free. When she rose that morning, it had seemed like a good idea to attend the lecture about record keeping for independent operators. Even if she didn't learn anything new, she'd hoped it would distract her thoughts. Images of Rae played in constant loop in her mind. She saw her mouth twisted with release as she came last night, and her body shuddering against the wall. And that woman, not Cori, on her knees in front of her, Rae's hands in her hair.

Not only did the seminar fail to dull the refrain, but the recycled air left her throat scratchy and dry. To top it off, the man in front of her smelled of mothballs and forgotten Fritos. When the speaker brought the session to a close by asking if there were any questions, Cori mentally threatened to dissect anyone who dared speak up. Thankfully no one needed another clarification and they were released. She sucked in a breath as she exited the room. The air was no less stale, but it was gloriously free from the smell of fried corn products.

She stopped short when she saw Rae leaning against the opposite wall, her expression at once guarded and pleading. Holding Cori's gaze, she straightened and walked slowly toward her. In the span of fifteen steps, Cori debated all the arguments against standing her ground and demanding an explanation for Rae's behavior. She had no claim on her. They'd had sex, that was all, and obviously their encounter meant nothing to Rae. But entitled or not, her heart screamed out its jealousy.

"Hi." Rae's sky blue eyes were cloudy and dark. Cori wondered if that's what guilt looked like on a player's face.

Of all the questions raging inside her head, the only word that made it past her lips was another, "Hi."

They stared at each other, stationary against the tide of

conventioneers. The seconds passed without a word, just the longing look on Rae's face holding Cori in place. Rae's mouth parted more than once, and nothing came out. She lifted her hand and cupped Cori's cheek. The soft pressure of her thumb burned a path over the planes of Cori's face. God help her, she relaxed into the touch and closed her eyes, allowing the sensation to momentarily chase away the track in her head.

"Spend the day with me?" Rae asked.

"I don't know."

Cori's insides knotted at the simple request. She should say no, take her books and her heart to her room, pack her clothes, and fly to Seattle early. It was the only safe thing to do. No rational person would choose to stay here and sort through the contradictory signals Rae kept giving her. But Rae's unexpected presence made it impossible to walk away. Cori wanted to know her motivation for being here. She wanted to peel back another layer and find out who Rae really was.

"Cori..." Rae glanced around, like if she looked hard enough, she'd find the words she was searching for written on the wall. "Sometimes I do stupid things."

Her hand slid down Cori's arm. Her fingers toyed with the tips of Cori's, but she didn't reach for more. Cori closed the gap, pulling Rae to her for a slow, exploring kiss. She traced the inside of Rae's mouth, searching for a leftover taste of the night before. She found nothing but the soft, warm slide of Rae's tongue against hers. Rae whimpered and sagged in her arms, a tremor just beneath the surface.

Cold air replaced Rae's lips before Cori was ready. What was it about this woman? She turned Cori inside out with a glance, a touch. The first day by the pool, the seduction had felt well rehearsed. Now, however, Cori got the distinct impression that Rae was flying blind, relying on instinct. She was asking for something more, but Cori didn't know what that was. As she took Rae's hand and followed her out of the casino, she doubted Rae knew either.

One thing was certain, she wanted to find out.

❖

According to the odometer in Rae's car, they'd traveled fifteen miles into the desert, leaving the strip behind. Cori relaxed in the passenger seat, Rae's hand on her thigh. The window was down and KT Tunstall played on the stereo.

"Where are you taking me?" Cori asked.

"Away from who I am." Rae's voice was distant and reflective. Smiling, she patted Cori's leg and pointed to a road sign. "We'll be at the Hoover Dam in about twenty minutes."

Cori wondered about Rae's answer. While she was clinging to bits and pieces, trying to discover the real Rae underneath the image, Rae seemed willing to abandon that part of herself she donned for the tourists, shedding it at the city limits.

"Where would you normally be right now, if you weren't here with me?" Cori asked. She hoped Rae was ready to share, if only just a little.

The face in the mirror smiled lazily back at her. "In class." Rae glanced at the clock in the dash. "Collective bargaining and public policy."

For Cori, who made her living through touch and intuition, the description did little to communicate what the class was about. "What's your major?"

Rae trailed her fingers idly over the inside seam of Cori's jeans. "Business management." She smiled, her eyes hidden behind her dark glasses. "I want the big office on the top floor."

The ambitious statement seemed at odds with the windblown woman in the driver's seat. Cori tried to picture Rae in a suit, all buttoned up and pin-striped. She could easily imagine her in the role of power dyke. Rae's sexy smile and easy confidence lent readily to the image.

"You'd give up the glamour of the casino floor?"

The answer was more important than Cori wanted to admit. Not that dealing blackjack was actually glamorous, as she'd implied. She knew the job wasn't, but the casino provided Rae with endless opportunities to meet new women. The thought sent a stab of jealousy through her. She wasn't entitled to feel possessive of Rae, and the emotion was irrational, but the burn in her gut owned her nonetheless.

"In a heartbeat." Rae's answer was automatic, like the decision had been made long ago and she was simply waiting for her plans to reach fruition.

She turned into a deserted gravel parking lot. The dam was nowhere in sight. If they were anywhere near the tourist attraction, the lot should be overflowing with cars and people.

"I thought we were going to Hoover Dam," Cori said.

Rae smiled. "We are."

Save for the constant drone of cars passing on the highway, the air around them was quiet. Cori listened more closely. The usual sounds of the city were absent, but underlying the buzz of wheels turning on pavement, there was something more, a rushing, roaring in the distance.

"Is that—"

"Yep." Rae hopped out of the car and circled around to Cori's door. "Coming?" she invited with an outstretched hand.

They fell in step together, Rae's arm resting on Cori's

shoulders. It felt good, with just the right hint of possessiveness. Cori sank into the feeling, allowing herself to be drawn down the path away from the car.

"What about you?" Rae asked. "I have no idea what you do for a living."

Could that be true? Cori searched her memory. She and Rae had spent shockingly little time talking, but still, she had to be aware of something so fundamental. Realization settled in. They knew nothing about each other. "I'm a massage therapist."

"That explains it." Rae looked at her like she wanted to eat her alive.

Cori stumbled. "Explains what?"

"Why you're so good with your hands." Rae's arm dropped to Cori's waist, holding her tightly. "I should have realized when I saw you at the convention center. I knew which group was meeting."

Cori felt her face flush. "I'll give you a real massage sometime, and then you can decide how good I am with my hands."

Rae glanced sideways at her. "You're blushing." She studied Cori more closely. "And very cute."

Cori stared at her lips, full and inviting. The need to know more about Rae burned away as she watched something change in her eyes. Her expression was serious, the usual sexy grin absent. In its place was a tenderness that made her seem so vulnerable Cori caught her breath. Rae leaned in close, her mouth hovering over Cori's for a moment, then she kissed her, slowly and deliberately. Red flares of desire curled through Cori, stretching out to engulf her. Her grip on Rae slackened, her hands falling to her side. She felt weak, aware of nothing but the hot press of their lips and the promise of fulfillment.

The simple touch was overwhelming, and the growing need that burned her insides raged up, demanding more. This connection was all she craved. The moment one encounter with Rae ended, her body simmered, yearning for the next.

Rae's lips brushed hers one final time and she linked their pinkies together and started walking again, drawing Cori with her. They followed the trail around a bend that opened to a clearing.

Cori had seen pictures of Hoover Dam, but nothing had prepared her for the vista stretched out below them. Water, cool and placid like liquid satin, pooled at the top, held back by a massive wall of concrete. Puget Sound, Cori's baseline comparison for bodies of water, was a dull grayish blue. The Colorado River, which fed the dam, was the kind of blue Cori had only ever found in Crayola boxes and, she realized, in Rae's eyes in the moment before she climaxed.

Rae's arms wrapped around her from behind. "The spillways are closed off right now, letting the water build up, but they'll open one soon. It's amazing."

Cori leaned into her, absorbed by the beauty of the surroundings and the heat flowing between them. "Thank you."

Rae snuggled closer. "For what?"

Cori turned and kissed her lightly on the cheek. "Sharing this with me. It's…" She searched for the right word to capture the moment, but they all sounded flat. "It's special." She shook her head. It was the best she could come up with.

"I'm glad you like it." Rae paused. "We could go closer. They have tours, complete with placards and guides who spout random facts about how much concrete was used to build the dam and how much water pressure is at the base."

Rae's uncertainty tugged at Cori. She liked that Rae was

struggling to impress her, to make the moment even more perfect than it already was. She regarded her seriously. "I like it here."

Rae lowered her head to kiss her again. Once more the image from the party the night before fluttered behind Cori's eyes, drawing a sharp sigh from her. Rae's touch shook loose the memory and as their lips met, Cori surrendered herself to the moment, opening herself to exploration. Rae started slow, keeping her arms around Cori's waist. Her tongue barely skimmed past Cori's teeth before retreating and returning for more. The timid control frustrated Cori. She knew Rae wanted more, she felt it in the air whenever Rae looked at her, but still she held back.

With a growl, Cori backed her against a tree and insinuated her thigh between Rae's legs. She demanded more and Rae finally responded. Her fingers tangled in Cori's hair and she tugged hard. A sharp edge of surprise shot through Cori as her throat was exposed. Molten heat built to pinpoint sharpness where Rae's mouth latched on to her pulse, bringing her soul screaming to the surface. This was the Rae she wanted. Hot and demanding. Hard enough to drive the thought, and the unwanted images, from her mind.

She gasped as Rae spun her with alarming speed, pinning her firmly to the tree. The bark dug into Cori's back, making her squirm. She felt Rae fighting with her buttons, scratching futilely against them as she reclaimed her mouth. Not willing to wait, Cori yanked her shirt free from her shorts and pushed Rae's hand against her skin, urging it up to her breasts.

The responsible part of her nagged that what she was doing was wrong, that she would never behave like this in Seattle. She was exposed in a place that, while it felt secluded, was very much public. She was *not* the kind of girl who fucked total strangers against a tree in the middle of the day. But

Rae wasn't a total stranger. Cori knew exactly what Rae was about. She was a player, interested only in a passing encounter, nothing more. And at that moment, that was enough. It had to be.

"God, you make me crazy." Rae pinched and twisted her nipples.

Fire shot from Cori's breasts to her clit, driving away the reasons for stopping. Apparently in Vegas, she was exactly this kind of girl. Not only did she want to be fucked against a tree in broad daylight, she wanted to do it *now.* She reached out for Rae, needing her closer, but Rae stepped back from her, hastily wiping her mouth. The shy tour guide look was back on her face, and she brushed Cori's clothes into place as a family of four emerged on the path.

Cori groaned. "You've got to be kidding me." She hadn't even heard the intruders approaching. Her skin burned and her clit screamed for more. Now.

"Sorry about that." Rae smiled like a teenager caught on her parents' couch, proud, embarrassed, and uncertain all at once.

From the hesitation in her eyes, Cori knew if she wanted this to continue, she would have to be the one to push for it. "We need to go back to my room."

She steered Rae back to the car, moving like a woman being chased. Before long, the memory of Rae coming in another woman's mouth would catch up with her again. But for now, she didn't want to surrender the sexual tension building between them to a jealousy she had no right to feel.

CHAPTER SEVEN

"Stop looking at me like that." Rae forced herself to stand on the opposite side of the elevator from Cori. She didn't trust herself to be any closer and if the damned car didn't start climbing the cable just a little faster, she was going to forget the fact that security, and therefore her boss, could see everything she did while on the property.

Cori lowered her eyelids sexily. "Like what?"

Her voice was huskier than usual and Rae faltered, almost forgetting her objection. "Like you don't care that there's a camera in this elevator recording everything we do."

Her skin burned under Cori's close scrutiny, and every time she met Cori's demanding gaze, her brain stuttered to a stop, leaving her wanting and vulnerable. All the reasons for not pursuing a relationship with Cori had been so clear the night before. But today, with Cori's bare skin only a few painfully slow floors away, those reasons were beyond her mental reach.

Cori looked pointedly at the camera and took a half-step toward her. "Is that why you're not touching me?"

"Yes."

The twin mirrored doors slid mercifully open at Cori's floor and Rae led her impatiently from the car. She entwined her fingers with Cori's as they walked down the hall, her thumb smoothing a path over the soft moon of skin on the back of Cori's hand.

Cori pressed her lips to Rae's cheek. "Today, at the dam, that was really special for me. Thank you."

The kiss was soft, unassuming, almost chaste. The sweetness of it clutched at Rae's heart and she wondered irrationally if she could shower without washing away the rose-petal-soft imprint of Cori's lips. The silly, teenage-girl thought startled her. She'd abandoned such romantic pining when she left high school, and even back then she hadn't experienced the mind-numbing pull of another person. She'd never felt so helpless to resist her desire for a woman.

The walk down the corridor seemed to take even longer than the ride in the elevator. To Rae's surprise, she didn't have to fight her hormones into submission. She truly wanted this experience to be different. A deep craving for connection with Cori made her want to go slow, to explore her completely and give her everything she wanted. Cori deserved to be worshipped, with Rae on her knees paying homage.

When they arrived at Cori's door, she squeezed Cori's hand, a gentle reassurance to help calm a tremble she felt. "Are you sure about this?"

The question sounded absurd to Rae's ears, but she had to ask. They'd spent the day together, navigating the boundaries with one another. She wanted Cori to know, more than anything else, that she *liked* her. She didn't see her as only sexy and wild and hot. She really liked the woman she was getting to know— her personality, her sensibility, her vulnerability. Incredibly, this night didn't have to end in sex for her to be completely happy. The day and the memories they were building were worth more to her than that. Cori was worth more.

"Yes, I'm sure." Cori handed her the key.

The symbolism wasn't lost on Rae. With a simple gesture, she'd been given the key to open Cori's world. All she had to do was step through the door. Was she brave enough to abandon the role she'd always played so well and lay claim to a new life, one that included Cori and all the promise she offered? Rae hesitated. Maybe she was giving too much significance to the moment. Perhaps all Cori wanted was for her to open the door, push her against the wall, and fuck her until she exploded. The latter would certainly be easier and more comfortable. Rae knew what to do in a world constructed of sex games and orgasms. Heartfelt connections were ethereal to her, something she'd have to stretch to obtain. God help her, Cori made her want to reach for happily ever after.

Thankfully the room was empty. The last thing Rae needed was the judgment of Cori's protective roommate. She leaned against the closed door and watched Cori loosen one button after another until her shirt hung open down the front, the lace of her bra peeking through. This was crazy and foolish and she didn't want to stop. Bands of panic tightened around her chest. The familiar thoughts that had driven her to run from Cori and find comfort with another woman crept in around the edges of her consciousness. The intensity of her emotions—her illogical, inexplicable, and certainly unwanted emotions—built to a crashing crescendo.

Cori couldn't possibly be feeling like this. Hell, Rae wasn't even sure what she felt, herself. The overwhelming tide could recede in a moment and leave her wet but no worse for the wear. She forced herself to remember that Cori would soon be leaving Vegas. Rae needed to accept that and take what she could from this moment despite the teasing sense of possibility. Tonight wasn't about building an unbreakable bond. It wasn't about forever. It was about sex. Really good sex with a really sexy woman. It couldn't be anything more.

Cori peeled off her clothes, one garment at a time, her eyes on Rae as she dropped them seductively to the floor. The more skin she revealed, the further out of control Rae's thoughts spiraled. She wanted her. Not just for the frantic press of their bodies, but in the seconds, minutes, hours, and everything that came afterward. She wanted to hold her and wake up next to her in the morning.

"There's something really wrong here." Cori's expression was teasing. She crossed to where Rae stood immobile against the door. "I'm naked and you still have all these clothes on."

Her kiss wasn't gentle, but it wasn't overwhelming. Cori didn't seem bent on domination. It was as though she was trying to pull Rae out of her thoughts and back into the moment. Rae felt the familiar chill of anticipation as Cori opened her shirt, only without the sense of urgency that always accompanied the prelude to sex. She reminded herself that she wasn't on her lunch hour. She was here, in Cori's room, with the entire night in front of them. She touched Cori's fingers, aiding them to push the shirt down her shoulders. The glide of Cori's fingers against her bare abdomen brought a ripple of tension that tripped over her body, chasing Cori's touch to her sports bra.

Cori removed this quickly, leaving Rae naked from the waist up. Saving two nights ago, Rae couldn't remember the last time she'd undressed fully for sex. What was the point when she invariably had to drag everything back on after a few minutes? She started as Cori circled her nipple with a finger. The touch was soft but far from timid. She took her time, exploring the contours of Rae's skin as it puckered and tightened, then letting her tongue follow her fingers. Rae slid her fingers through Cori's hair, holding tight, prolonging the moment as ribbons of desire rippled through her.

Cori worked her hand down Rae's abdomen, pausing at the waistband of her jeans before pushing forward. When her fingers skimmed Rae's clit, Rae moaned at the touch, but held Cori's wrist firm, refusing to let her go further. She had to slow the momentum. It felt too much like their last encounter. In spite of the heat in Cori's touch, and her eyes and mouth, Rae wanted more. She didn't want to fuck. She wanted to make love.

She drew Cori up and kissed her gently. "Slow down. Let me get undressed."

Cori moaned. "God, I want you so much." She buried her face in the curve of Rae's neck. "Why are you doing this to me?"

Rae unzipped herself and pushed her jeans and panties down her hips. Cori's hand stayed between her thighs and her finger twitched, just barely. The sensation was enough to make Rae jerk back, pressing her ass against the door.

"I want you, too," she groaned. "But I want us to take our time and enjoy one another." She worked her way out of her shoes then kicked her pants aside. "Come on." She took Cori's hand and led her to the bed.

The air between them was heavy and thick as she slid back the covers and lowered Cori onto the bed. She held her body above Cori's, not touching, barely breathing, scared to move forward with her intentions. Light from the neon night filtered in around the edges of the drapes, making it bright enough to see the dark desire smoldering in Cori's eyes but leaving the planes of her face and body etched in shadows. Rae traced the line between light and dark from the base of Cori's throat down to the apex of her thighs, dipping into the moisture pooled there. Cori held herself rigid, trembling at the touch. She sucked in a ragged breath when Rae slid further, letting her fingers brush Cori's clit.

Bracing herself with her arms on either side of Cori's head, she lowered herself until their bodies were touching. The graze of their skin was light at first. A trembling electric pulse arced between them, compelling more. Rae took a deep, steadying breath and focused. She wanted to remember everything about this moment. The deep, dark desire threatening to drown her in Cori's eyes. The tremor in her arms. The building throb pulsing inside her, and the growing pool of moisture between her legs. The tickle of Cori's pubic hair blending with her own. She gazed down at the fan of Cori's hair against the pillow and the slow trickle of sweat beading down her neck. The beat of her pulse stirred just below the surface of her skin, pleading for Rae's lips.

When she could no longer hold herself back, she sank down the rest of the way until their bodies molded together. They settled into slow, undulating thrusts as Cori's hips rose up, circling and drawing Rae down, not pushing for release, but dancing beneath her. The seductive rhythm urged Rae to take her, but she stayed with Cori, not increasing the tempo. She rode the wave as it took them higher, still refusing to meet the request for more. The night had just begun and she wanted to prove that she could wait.

Cori lifted her head to capture Rae's mouth in a kiss. The sucking, sliding invitation of her tongue drew Rae in, demanding only that she surrender herself to pleasure. Every kiss should be like this, she thought, bringing the rest of the world to a stop in its warm, erotic give-and-take.

When they finally released each other enough to breathe, Rae leaned on one elbow and stroked Cori's swollen lips with her thumb. Awed and humbled that this beautiful woman was willing to share herself so freely, Rae pressed her lips to Cori's eyes, one after the other. "You're so beautiful. Why are you here with me?"

The question nagged at her. When all other thought fled her, that one thought remained. What had she done to deserve this perfect moment with Cori? What could she do to make it last?

"I could ask you the same question." Cori met Rae's probing gaze. "But I won't. I'm just going to enjoy you while you're here."

Her choice of words puzzled Rae. Cori was the one who was leaving, not Rae. Was she only interested in a fleeting encounter? Maybe Rae had misjudged the situation. She was certain, after the look she'd intercepted at the party, that Cori was jealous and hurt. Had she since decided that Rae wasn't worth more than a vacation fling? Rae was starting to want much more than that but didn't dare think about the reasons. She certainly wasn't ready to share her confusing emotions.

"Then let's enjoy ourselves." She ran her tongue along the edge of Cori's ear and sucked the lobe between her teeth. She bit down, but only with a teasing pressure. Tonight wasn't about testing the edge between pleasure and pain. She just wanted Cori to feel treasured.

Normally she knew exactly where to go, what to touch, how to touch, whether to use her hand, her mouth, her thigh. Tonight she wanted to do everything all at once. Of all her options, however, she wasn't willing to sacrifice the connection she felt when she looked into Cori's eyes. She ran her hand down Cori's body, smoothing it over the small goose bumps rising on her skin. She paused to enjoy the tension in her tight abdominal muscles, fanning her fingers over the slight swell of her tummy. Cori was soft and yielding, and Rae continued down, not stopping until she reached the hot, wet folds of her sex. She felt Cori tense beneath her touch and saw a yearning in the depths of her eyes that barely made it to her lips.

"Please, Rae. Don't make me wait." It was the faintest whisper, a prayer between rough, shallow breaths.

She was so wet and so open. Carefully, slowly, Rae

pushed into her. She almost cried out at the perfection of the moment. She could see the need and hunger written plainly on Cori's face, feel it in the tightening muscles surrounding her fingers. It was impossible to hold back any longer. Cori didn't want to wait, either, so Rae did the only thing left to her. She took her with the careful abandon of a lover. She wanted, no *needed* to possess her, to take everything she offered and give her everything she deserved.

Cori felt perfect, the surge and pulse of her, the gliding sweat on her skin, the clutching need of her nails digging into Rae's back. She rose up to meet every stroke, thrusting against Rae. Eyes closed, head tilted back, she released a long, rising groan as her muscles clenched and fluttered in release.

Rae clutched her, sure in the aftermath of Cori's orgasm that she'd never really seen a woman before. Not like that. No matter how many times she'd experienced a shared orgasm, she'd never looked into the soul of a woman as she released herself so completely in the woman's hands. Rae was humbled and honored to have Cori open herself up this way. She ached to keep this moment locked in time, a brief reprieve from the harshness of life. Was this what a future with Cori would hold? She felt herself slipping further down a path of promises and commitment.

Cori sagged against the bed. "God, you're good at that."

She sucked in air and waited for the blur of black and white pinpoint dots to clear the edges of her vision. She hated that she needed Rae so much. It would be simpler, less complicated, and less painful if she didn't. She knew she should have said no when Rae asked to spend the day with her. She should have said no when Rae kissed her as they looked out over the dam. And when Rae brought her back to the hotel. But how could she? Hell, it was her idea to come here. And why not?

If only she were able to enjoy the physical pleasure of

being with Rae and ignore the clawing emotional need, the overwhelming sadness of knowing she soon had to leave, and the scratching jealousy that Rae would probably be in another woman's arms before her plane touched down in Seattle. She'd been in another woman's arms when Cori found her last night. She'd tried all day to suppress the memory of that blonde on her knees bringing Rae to climax with her mouth. But no matter how forcefully she ignored it, the truth of the situation didn't change. Rae was a player, a woman only interested in her next conquest.

Cori didn't want to believe it. When Rae was with her, she felt special, like she was the only woman in the world, more importantly, the only woman in *Rae's* world. But that was wishful thinking. In spite of her better judgment, Cori snuggled into Rae's arms. Just like last time, she felt safe and protected. She hadn't realized how important that feeling was to her.

Her father had taught her not to expect comfort in the arms of another. His "my way or the highway" approach to parenting was unforgiving, and through years of absolutes, Cori had learned to be self-reliant. Maricel, her oldest sister, said it hadn't always been like that. She remembered their father being loving and nurturing. He'd changed when his own father died, his passion and love of family apparently buried along with the cherished man. His heart never seemed to recover. Cori didn't know if it was true. All she remembered was steely eyes condemning her at every turn.

As she grew up, it was odd to see her friends being hugged and encouraged. She was grateful to avoid being scolded. Her mother had been too busy cleaning house and bowing to his wishes to stop him from chasing their children out of their lives. Latino families were known for living together long after the children reached adult status. Cori, on the other hand, had moved out of her parents' house the day she turned eighteen. She seldom visited anymore. She could live without the sense that she was a disappointment.

Rae kissed the top of her head. "I love the way you look. Wild, tense, chasing the moment of release. Makes me want to try harder, take you higher." Her tone was reflective. She squeezed Cori a little tighter. "You make everything else just disappear. Everything that is normally important to me just fades away."

Cori didn't respond right away, letting Rae's words settle in her brain. She was saying all the right things. Did she say that to every woman she was with? Cori sighed. Why couldn't she just relax and enjoy the moment? "Do you mean that?"

"Yeah." Rae traced random patterns over her hip. "Scares me to death."

"Why?" Cori couldn't believe she asked the question. It betrayed her need to hope that maybe there was a chance with Rae after all. She needed to not entertain that possibility, even for a second. They lived hours apart, in different area codes for Christ's sake. Rae had already demonstrated that, when it came to women, impulse control was not her strong point. Only a naïve fool would ever trust her.

"How could it not scare me?" Rae sought her eyes. "I don't let women affect me like this, but here I am, trying to make sense of the hold you have on me. I don't understand it, but it's still there."

"And that's bad?"

"Cori, I don't even know where you live. I know nothing about you, except that you're great with your hands, your voice melts my insides, and when you kiss me everything else disappears."

Cori smiled. All she had to do to keep Rae's focus was to

kiss her? Too easy. She pressed her lips to Rae's, pleased with the sharp intake of breath as she pushed her tongue past Rae's teeth. She didn't lose herself in the kiss like she had earlier. Rather, she just wanted to test the truth in Rae's statement. The glossed-over state of her eyes told her everything she needed to know.

"Seattle."

Rae blinked. "Huh?"

"I live in Seattle."

"Do you like it there?"

That was something Cori seldom thought about. What difference did it make if she liked it or not? It was where she lived, where she worked, where her family lived. She'd never had any reason not to like it. "I guess."

Rae looked disappointed, like someone let the air out of her. "Do you sing there?"

That's right, Rae had said something earlier about her singing and she'd missed it in the wake of the kissing comment. When had Rae heard her sing? Cori tried to remember their car ride. Had she sung along with the car stereo? She didn't think so.

"No, not unless you count karaoke."

She must have looked puzzled because Rae explained, "I stopped in during the auditions yesterday."

"Oh." With the emotional storm surrounding Rae, she'd forgotten all about the audition. "I was a little drunk. Those blue drinks they serve by the pool have more rum than blue."

"Think you'll get the gig?" There was an odd note in Rae's voice.

Cori studied her closely and realized what she was seeing. Rae was fearful. Players didn't like their throwaway partners to show up again. No doubt she was worried that if Cori joined the band she would move to town and expect them to pick up where they left off. Her unspoken dismay made Cori's throat close.

"Kel said they aren't going to make a decision for a couple of weeks," she explained, saddened that Rae obviously didn't want her to get the job. "They're going on vacation, then when they get back they'll let everybody know."

She sensed Rae growing tenser as the conversation went on and felt a wave of anger rise from her belly. Did the thought that she might move to Vegas upset Rae that much? Was she worried that Cori would try to stake a claim over her or tie her down?

"Do you want to get it?" Rae asked.

Cori didn't look at her. "Don't worry. If I decide to move here, I'll try not to cramp your style."

The hand caressing Cori's hip stopped moving. "What does that mean?"

"I saw you with that woman last night, Rae. I know what you're like." Cori willed her mouth to stop moving, but she couldn't stop the words from forming. Even from her point of view, it felt like she was attacking Rae, but she couldn't help herself.

Rae reared back. "What the hell are you talking about?"

"At the party. I know you saw me."

"So?"

Cori's temper flashed. "*So*, I don't want to be with a woman who fucks *me* in the afternoon and another woman the same night."

Rae was out of bed, hands on her hips, outrage lining her face. "Who I fuck is none of your damn business." She jerked her pants on. "And I didn't hear any complaints from you when I made you come."

The words stung. How could it not be any of Cori's

business? Rae had just told her she was special and Cori *knew* she meant it. How could it not matter if Rae gave that part of herself to another woman?

Cori jumped out of bed. "It goddamn well is my business. For just plain old-fashioned health concerns, if nothing else." She punctuated the sentence with short little jabs to Rae's chest with her forefinger.

"No, Cori, it's not. You are not my wife. I can fuck who I want, when I want." Rae shoved her arms into the sleeves of her shirt, leaving the buttons open. She scooped up her shoes and opened the door. "I like you, Cori. A lot. But you don't get to tell me what to do and how to live. We haven't even known each other for a week."

Panic gathered in Cori's chest. A few minutes ago they'd been so close, and with the night stretching out before them, she'd imagined a deepening of the connection she'd sensed earlier, at the dam. She wished she could take back the last few minutes. Even as she'd spoken, she knew she was taking a risk and that her words would push Rae away. Maybe that was why she did it. Rae was only going to hurt her if given the chance. At least this way she wouldn't have that power.

Cori remained silent as she watched Rae walk out the door. The urge to run after her was so strong that she grabbed hold of the bed to stop her feet from moving. The events of the past day or so would only sting for a short time. Then she would be free of Rae's hold on her mind and body, free to live the life she planned without complications. One day she would find someone who would share her dreams and become part of her world. Rae Sutherland wasn't that woman.

CHAPTER EIGHT

Rae straightened the knot in her tie for the thirtieth time that night. Not that it needed straightening; she executed a perfect double Windsor every time she donned her work uniform. Rather, she needed something to do while the shuffler whirred through three decks before she could deal the next round.

Cori stood at the roulette table, just beyond the reach of her voice, but well within her range of sight. Her presence was the kind of distracting torture Rae didn't need while working. The normal buffet of women filtering through the casino damaged her concentration less than Cori did, all by herself. Normally, Rae would engage a woman from across the room, letting her gestures transmit her intentions. She would remain focused on the table in front of her, but section off a little pocket of excitement in her mind, one that would get her full attention later.

With Cori, she couldn't bring her thoughts in line. All she could picture was the hurt on her face, first at the party, then last night as Rae walked out of her room. Twice she'd caused pain and was angry with herself for doing so. Cori had forgiven her the first time. Would she do it a second? Just seeing her, even without being able to talk to her, gave Rae comfort. At least she was still in Vegas. There was a chance that they could spend time together again.

"Distracted much, Rae?"

"Christ." She just about jumped out of her skin when Marco touched her arm. "Don't do that."

He pointed to the silent shuffler. "Cards are ready."

Reflexively, she began laying out cards for the next round. There were two empty chairs at her table. They'd been full when she'd placed the new decks in the shuffler. The players had left without her noticing. Taking cover behind a veil of cool efficiency, she finished out the hand, paying out one winner and collecting losses from the other three.

"Greg wants to count out your table. It's time for you to take a break." Marco spoke softly in her ear, low enough that the gamblers wouldn't hear.

Rae asked the players if they'd like to color up before she closed the table, then decked the house chips out on trays as Greg arrived to take over. It wasn't unusual to count down a table mid-shift. Random spot-checks on accuracy were a part of the casino's routine loss prevention efforts, aimed at keeping dealers focused and honest.

Marco waited with her while they verified the funds. "What's going on with you?"

Rae tore her eyes off Cori. "What do you mean?"

"I've been watching you ignore every hot woman in the place, including the ones sending signals. That's not like you."

This was not good. Rae always noticed good-looking women. *Always.* Even when she was getting over the flu a year ago she'd noticed a particularly tasty blonde with legs that went on forever. She'd gone to the guest's room after the shift and let her kiss away her pains.

"I don't know what you're talking about," she said, glancing back to see if Cori was watching. She wasn't.

The banker signaled that everything checked out and Marco walked her toward the break area and away from Cori. "Come on, Rae. Cut the bullshit."

Rae tried a different tactic. "School is a pain, man. Midterms are kicking my ass this quarter. Seriously. Nothing to worry about."

Marco didn't look convinced. He motioned for her to sit as he lifted a plastic container from the refrigerator. "Loti made tamales."

He put the container, sans lid, in the microwave while Rae found a couple of bottles of water. Food was Marco's solution for everything, bless him. Not a bad approach to life, really. Hard to not find common ground over a good plate of gazpacho.

"Eat." He dropped a portion in front of Rae and handed her a fork.

It wasn't that she didn't want to unburden herself, she just didn't know what to say. How could she explain to a stand-up guy like Marco what she was feeling for Cori when she didn't understand it herself? He'd been happily married the entire time Rae had known him and was singular in his devotion to his wife and their children. He was the guy who helped little old ladies cross the street, played catch with his kids in the yard, and dressed his family up for church on Sunday. He didn't do those things because he had to, and he didn't seem to regret giving up his single life like some guys. Rae had concluded that taking care of others made him feel like more of a man. And that he could do it for the woman he loved made life all the sweeter.

Rae wondered how much easier life would be if she were

like him. She chewed the layers of corn and pork slowly, savoring the flavor and trying to assemble her thoughts into a cohesive summary to present to him. For his part, Marco ate in silence, giving her the room she needed. The tamale went down easy before she finally decided to ask his opinion.

"How did you know that Loti was the one?" It seemed like a good place to start and hopefully find the answer to her real question: How would she know if Cori was the right one for her?

Marco's smile said that only an idiot wouldn't know the answer to that question. Which, Rae reasoned, didn't feel too far off base. She'd spent a good deal of time in the last few days feeling properly idiotic.

"That was easy," he said. "When I met Loti, I stopped noticing all the other women. Or, if I did notice, I couldn't help comparing them to her."

"Oh." This was not going to help. Rae needed someone to tell her she was acting crazy and had to get herself under control. Still, she couldn't help but ask for more information. "What did you do?"

"I begged her to marry me."

No surprises there. Of course he'd just known and done the respectable thing. A guy like Marco bought a ring and got down on one knee. He knew how to count his blessings. "How long did you know her first?"

"Four days."

Rae choked on her water, sending it sputtering across the room. "What?"

"I had to do something fast. She was engaged to another man and she was going to move to Georgia to be with him. I knew I couldn't live without her."

"You made her choose."

"I couldn't ask her to give up her future unless I promised something just as good in return," Marco said. "So I offered her all I had."

Rae couldn't conceive of taking a risk like that, or making such a profound promise. But when she was with Cori she wasn't so certain. Anything seemed possible. "How did you know you could keep that promise?"

Marco shrugged. "I just knew."

Rae stared down at her empty plate. Was it possible to know about forever after only four days? Maybe for someone like Marco. She would need longer than that to make any kind of real commitment. Hell, maybe she'd never be able to make such a serious promise. There was only one way to find out, and Cori was the first woman who'd made her consider the possibility.

Right now Cori was out there watching a little white ball circle the roulette wheel, while Rae was sitting here feeling sorry for herself. If she wanted something good to happen, she couldn't keep waiting for it to come to her. She needed to be the one to take a chance.

"I've got to go." She stood. "Thanks, Marco. For everything."

Rae didn't stop to think about what she would say, what she *should* say, as she walked up to Cori. She was afraid that any kind of hesitation would stop her cold. All the same, when those smoldering dark eyes lifted to her, she wished she'd taken a moment to prepare herself.

"Hi." She almost stammered.

Cori ignored the greeting and turned her attention back to the roulette table without a word. She sat a stack of chips on black seventeen.

Rae's vocal cords ground to a halt. She wasn't used to

being given the cold shoulder. Women responded to her and sought her out. Cori's obvious disdain set her adrift in new territory and Rae didn't enjoy feeling lost.

Falling back on time-tested technique, she stepped in and placed her hand lightly on Cori's back. She moved her mouth next to Cori's ear and paused. She could feel Cori's body responding. Her breathing increased ever so slightly and a light tremor worked its way up her spine. Cori may not want to talk to her, but her body still craved Rae's touch.

Encouraged by the unconscious response, she said, "I've got another fifteen minutes on my lunch." Cori's body stiffened. Unsure if that was a good or bad sign, Rae continued, keeping her voice low and intimate. "Care to join me?"

Cori scooped up her chips and wheeled around, outrage and steam rising off her. "No, Rae. I don't want to join you." Her words flew out with tight, clipped precision, gaining momentum as she spoke. "I don't want to be yet another woman to follow you willingly to a supply closet…a *supply closet*, because you're too busy to fit in more than a few minutes on your lunch break. I don't want to be another name on your list of conquests, but it's too late for that I suppose."

She pushed past Rae, her eyes glistening, the fire fading from her words.

Rae chased after her, stopping her just before she reached the elevator. "What *do* you want, Cori? Tell me."

"Nothing." Cori shook her head for emphasis. "You can't give me what I want."

Rae wanted to argue, to be the kind of person Marco was, someone able to promise forever after four days and mean it. But she couldn't. It wasn't something she was capable of. Cori was right. She couldn't give her what she wanted. Hell, she didn't even know *what* Cori wanted. She might never know. Cori would leave in a few days and the way things were going,

Rae would never hear from her again. She couldn't let that happen.

Searching for a way to buy more time, she said, "We need to slow down. Please, Cori. Let's back up."

She could see the clock on the wall over Cori's head. Lunch would be over in just a few moments but she didn't care if she was late or not. Fixing things with Cori was more important.

"There's nothing to slow down, Rae. You made that abundantly clear last night." Cori stabbed her thumb at the elevator buttons.

"I'm sorry. I was an asshole." Rae pushed a hand through her hair. "You've got me so damned wound up and confused I don't know which way is up. All I know for sure is that the thought of never seeing you again is making me sick."

"Why?" Cori's voice was ice-cold to match the look in her eyes. "You have a rotating pool of women lining up for a chance to spend thirty minutes with you. And there are some things I'm not willing to share. The sooner I go back to Seattle, the better. For both of us."

It was a perfectly logical argument and Rae couldn't dispute it. But she also couldn't agree. The very thought made her chest ache. "I don't know how to explain. I can't get it all sorted out in my head. I just know how I feel."

Rae couldn't believe the words coming out of her mouth. She was confessing to a need she couldn't define and couldn't shake. Normally she kept her emotions in a tidy container somewhere in the back of her mind. She was aware of them, but she certainly didn't allow them free rein. Her life was controlled, logical, and on track. Work and school took priority. She was driven and focused on her career. She had never let anyone distract her from that. Until now.

Now she was skipping classes, intentionally returning late

to her shift, and had ignored a stream of women all day long. All for Cori. Why wasn't that enough? Why did Cori want her to lock up her libido and hand over the key? They'd only known each other for a few days. Cori had no right to expect that kind of sacrifice. Rae didn't owe fidelity to someone she'd just met, and she didn't owe Cori an apology for that. But here she was, ready to beg her forgiveness.

"Cori, listen, about Vicky—"

"Puleeze." Cori cut her off mid-sentence. "I don't want to know her *name*."

She wasn't going to make this easy. Rae tried again. "I'm sorry."

"What, Rae? What are you sorry for?"

Rae didn't respond. The answer seemed self-evident.

"Are you sorry I saw you? Sorry that you did it? Sorry that I cared? Sorry that you used her? Sorry that you used me? Sorry that you won't be fucking me again?" Cori advanced on Rae, her eyes dark and thundering. "Tell me, Rae, what *exactly* are you sorry for?"

That was a good question. Was she sorry about having sex with Vicky? She didn't know. She'd had sex with lots of women. Was she suddenly supposed to be sorry about her entire sexual history? Mostly she was sorry that she'd somehow hurt Cori. She couldn't stand that anything she did upset her. Still, she didn't think that was the answer Cori was looking for.

She held out her hands, palms up in supplication. "I'm sorry for everything." And she was. If she could take back that interlude with Vicky, she would, and not just because Cori was angry with her.

Cori sagged against the wall. "I know I'm being irrational and unreasonable." She spoke more to herself than to Rae. "I'm acting like a damn crazy woman, but I can't help it. The sight of that woman on her knees in front of you." She raised her eyes to meet Rae's. "Knowing that it was her mouth, not mine." Her voice faded and she looked away. "It was so infuriating. And...sexy. I couldn't stop watching. I had to stay and watch you come, but I wanted it to be me. Not her. I can't explain it."

Wow. Rae's head spun as Cori shared the experience from her point of view. She had no idea how much the encounter had affected her, or that there was more to her reaction than just jealousy and anger.

"I wanted it to be you," Rae confessed in a whisper. "It wasn't working at all until I pictured you. That's when everything exploded. And I opened my eyes and there you were. I thought for sure I was imagining you. Until you ran."

They stood in silence for several minutes. The conversation was too much for Rae to absorb. All she knew was that she'd said enough to prove she was losing her mind. Yet Cori was still with her, if only for a few more minutes. She didn't want to screw that up.

"What now?" she finally dared to ask.

Cori shook her head. "I have no idea."

Rae gathered Cori's hand in hers and brought it to her lips. After gently kissing the fingertips, she held it to her chest. "Spend the day with me tomorrow."

She had thought about asking if Cori would join her after work, but she didn't want to push her luck. She wanted Cori to know that she was searching for more than just her next orgasm. And she needed Cori to see her as more than just a sexual partner.

Cori smiled. "Really?"

"Yeah." Rae mentally ran through her plan for the day. She had obligations, but nothing Cori couldn't share, if she was willing. "It's Sunday. No school, no work. But I promised my mom I'd help her with some stuff around her house. You could join us."

The casual offer was tinged with uncertainty. She couldn't hide the way Cori affected her. Somehow in just a few days she had derailed Rae's intentions, shaking them up and handing them back in a complete jumble.

"Please," she added more seriously. "I'd like it a lot."

Rae's offer definitely wasn't what Cori had expected. Even during their afternoon at Hoover Dam, she constantly seemed to be working toward her next seduction. She would act shy and uncertain, but beneath it all, Cori sensed she was marking the time until she could get her into bed again. After the quarrel they'd just had, how would it be to spend the day with her and her mom?

Cori let the idea stay with her for a few moments. They'd finally admitted to feelings that weren't easy to understand. She didn't know what to make of Rae's sudden candor, or even whether she could trust what she was hearing. Rae had said she couldn't reach an orgasm the other night until she'd imagined Cori's mouth on her. That knowledge excited Cori but also confused her, a reaction she needed a lot more time to process.

Tomorrow seemed far away, especially considering she was leaving Las Vegas the day after, on Monday. She wanted to invite Rae up to her room now but didn't think she could handle intimate contact hot on the heels of their shared emotions. She needed to get to know Rae outside of the bedroom. And she needed to find out if Rae could see her as more than a sexual conquest. That Rae had extended the invitation spoke volumes, far more than her forced apology and subsequent revelations.

Cori watched the minutes pass on the wall clock and kept

waiting for Rae to announce that she had to go, but still, she stayed. It was time to release her before she lost her job.

"What time should I expect you in the morning?"

"Is that a yes? You'll spend the day with me?" Rae looked like she was ready to hop up and down with excitement.

"I don't think it's a good idea." Cori paused, trying to understand why she had agreed. She couldn't pull her thoughts together enough to analyze her reasons. Finally she conceded, "But yes, I'll spend the day with you."

"You won't regret it." Rae gave her a hug that was disappointingly brief and impersonal. "I promise."

Cori watched her run back to the pit. She moved easily, as if the tension had drained from her body. Cori was glad she'd had that effect, but her contentment worried her. A relationship with Rae would be logistically difficult unless she joined the band and moved to Vegas. And even if she did, there was no guarantee of anything lasting. The risk of gambling on a woman like Rae was obvious. People didn't change. Rae hadn't pretended to be anything she wasn't. And even if she really did have some feelings for Cori, how long would they last? Cori was only signing up for heartache if she allowed Rae in.

Releasing the breath she was holding, she made herself relax. Everything was going to be okay. She would enjoy tomorrow, and then she knew what she had to do. Saying a final good-bye wouldn't be easy, but Rae was who she was and Cori was too realistic to pretend she could turn her into something else. Even if Rae wasn't sure what she really wanted, Cori had no doubt. They weren't on the same page, and they never would be.

CHAPTER NINE

The light pink paper crinkled in Rae's hand and she smoothed the edges with her fingers. She felt silly carrying the bouquet of tulips and lilies up to Cori's room, but she always took fresh cut flowers on her Sunday visits. Her mom's one great regret about living in the desert was that gardens didn't flourish with the same burst of color, spring or not, as in the rest of the country. So Rae tried to take her a seasonal bouquet on a regular basis. Granted, that didn't mean she had to do the same for Cori, but she wanted to avoid awkwardness. Cori would notice the flowers on the backseat and wonder if they were for her. She might feel put out that Rae had only purchased lovely blooms for her mother. That was what she told herself until the door opened and Cori's eyes lit up.

"They're beautiful." She buried her face in the red and yellow blossoms and inhaled.

Rae felt the blood rushing to her face and hoped her tan would hide the blush. She'd never bought flowers for a woman, other than her mom. She didn't know what to expect, but Cori's reaction was perfect. She dragged Rae through the door by her lips. Not the greeting she'd expected after their heated argument the night before, but she wasn't about to complain.

"I'm glad you like them." The sentiment was a gross understatement, but her brain couldn't come up with anything else.

Cori looked around the room. "I don't have anything to put them in."

"Oh." Rae cursed the oversight. "I don't know what I was thinking."

In fact, she knew exactly what she'd been thinking. She wanted Cori to like her again. Simple. Practicalities, like a vase, had escaped her. She searched the room and offered the plastic ice bucket as a possibility. "How about this?"

Cori held the bouquet in front of her like a baton, or possibly a trophy, as she walked into the bathroom. She ran some water into the container and arranged the blooms carefully. Her fingers lingered on a waxy red tulip petal. "No one's ever given me flowers. It's quite...lovely. A real..."

"Surprise?" Rae suggested with faint cynicism.

"What I meant was that I didn't expect anything so... romantic."

Rae hesitated. Flowers *were* romantic, and given what they usually meant, the offering seemed unexpected to her as well. She smiled and shrugged, sure her blush was obvious now. "I don't know what to say."

Cori kissed her lightly on the lips. "Don't say anything. This is perfect as is."

They stood, lost in each other, until the sound of the door being opened startled them into motion. Julie, looking worse for the party she'd attended the night before, stood in the entrance, her gaze moving from Cori to Rae, to the vase of flowers, then back to Cori.

"I'm interrupting."

"No, we were just leaving." Cori kissed her on the cheek and led Rae from the room.

"Be good," Julie called after them. Then laughed.

❖

The drive to Rae's mom's passed quickly with Cori sitting quietly, apparently lost in thought. She didn't comment on the bundle sitting in the backseat. If it bothered her that Rae had bought flowers for her mother as well, she didn't mention it.

"Anything I should know about your mom before we get there?" she asked as they entered an older neighborhood in North Las Vegas. The houses here were built wind-tough to protect against unpredictable desert storms.

Plenty, Rae thought. For instance, her mom had no idea Cori was joining them. Rae hadn't thought to tell her. "Well, she's lived in Vegas her whole life. She has an unbelievable collection of Dean Martin records, and she thinks I can do no wrong."

"You must be the youngest kid." Cori's face was serene and her tone innocent.

"Why, do I seem spoiled?" Rae parked in the driveway and remarked uneasily, "This is it."

The laughter in Cori's eyes relaxed her a little bit, but she couldn't help the knot of tension in her stomach. She was nervous. She'd never brought a girlfriend home to meet her mom. *Girlfriend.* The word brought Rae up short. When exactly had she applied that term to Cori? Furthermore, what would Cori think if she knew? Giving her new emotions room to breathe was proving more confusing than she would have thought. Life was simpler when she knew, with the certainty of unemotional detachment, what the outcome of her actions would be.

Cori placed her hand on Rae's arm, stopping her from exiting the car. "Rae, I don't know why you're doing this, but thank you. It means a lot to me that you would bring me here."

"Yeah?" Rae raised one eyebrow, too nervous to pull off cool. "I'm glad."

She didn't add that she would've spent the day doing just about anything, including fire-walking or eating actual mud pies, to enjoy Cori's company for just a little longer. Hell, she might have even attended the Republican National Convention if Cori asked her to.

With her mom's bouquet under one arm, and holding Cori's hand, Rae waited at the door. Normally she would use her key, but with Cori along, that didn't seem like the right thing to do. She tried for a casual smile as she heard her mom unlocking the door. If Norma Sutherland was surprised that Rae wasn't alone, she didn't let it show. She swept them both inside, dropped a kiss on Rae's cheek, and introduced herself to Cori without skipping a beat.

"It's nice to meet you, Mrs. Sutherland."

"No, sweetie, call me Norma." She led them into the kitchen and took a vase from the pantry. "Mrs. Sutherland was an old dragon of a woman who terrorized my life." She winked. "God rest her soul."

"Mom never liked her mother-in-law," Rae explained, avoiding her own feelings about her grandmother.

"*Ex* mother-in-law, I'll thank you to remember."

Pearl Sutherland had been a difficult woman during her lifetime, demanding, harsh, and more than a little unforgiving. But Rae had chased after her love. Her grandmother was the only thing left in Vegas of the absentee father Rae barely remembered. Eventually, their relationship had grown to one of mutual tolerance, if not outright familial love. Her grandmother had taught her a lot about discipline, dedication, and hard work, and it had pleased her when Rae took to the lessons with a fervor sorely lacking in her only son.

Rae's relationship with her had been a complicated dance of mutual antagonism and protective admiration. At once proud and condemning of her, Pearl was seemingly incapable of saying "good job" without following the compliment with advice on how to do better next time. Rae didn't know how to explain the emotional soup surrounding her memories of her grandmother. Cori already looked shell-shocked without hearing the details. Norma had that effect on people.

"You girls thirsty? I have some iced tea in the fridge. Rae, get Cori a glass."

Rae did as she was told but resisted when they were ushered toward the table. If they sat down, her mom would spend the day grilling Cori rather than completing the chores she had lined up. Rae couldn't imagine any task less pleasant than listening to her mom tell Cori about the time she caught her kissing Jessie Parker in their tree house. Or, worse, she would probably love showing Cori pictures of three-year-old Rae blowing bubbles in the back yard, bare-ass naked.

"Mom, what's on the agenda today?"

Norma finished snipping her flowers and organizing them in the vase. "Cleaning. You sure you girls want to spend the day cooped up in that dusty room?" She directed the question to Cori.

"It sounds perfect to me…Norma."

Rae could think of a hundred other things she'd rather do, and most of them involved Cori naked and panting. "We're your willing servants, Mom. Show us what you need done."

Cori took another sip of the iced tea she hadn't finished and started up the stairs at Norma's urging. Rae smiled after her, musing at her good fortune. Very few women would choose to spend a day of their vacation cleaning out someone else's junk room. She started to follow, but her mom held her back.

"What's going on, sweetie?"

Rae feigned innocence. She wasn't ready to have this conversation. "What do you mean?"

The shift in Norma's face was almost imperceptible. The lines didn't alter, her smile didn't fade. Everything just... hardened. "Don't bullshit me. Tell me what that girl is doing here or I'll march upstairs and ask her myself."

Rae smiled bitterly. Her mom didn't fuck around when she wanted answers. "I don't know, Mom. She's a guest at the casino and I like her." She shrugged, trying to soften the importance of her words. She couldn't dwell on their significance for too long or she'd drown trying to sort it all out.

Norma's face softened. "Really?"

Rae glanced up the stairs, checking to see if Cori was listening. She debated holding back, not giving her mom any more information. In the end, she couldn't do that. Norma had always been there for her, taken care of her, pushed her to do better, and held her when it hurt. "Actually, I like her a lot, and I'm scared to death."

Norma patted her arm. "Sweetie, you were always so serious about everything, unwilling to take a chance unless you knew the cards would fall in your favor. Sometimes you have to let go." She smiled, the edges tight, almost sorrowful. "You deserve to be happy. I hope you can let it happen."

She left Rae standing alone at the bottom of the stairs wondering how something that sounded so simple could be so complicated. Just let it happen. That was all she had to do but, God help her, she didn't know what *it* was and she wasn't sure if she was strong enough to trust the unknown.

❖

Cori stood on the top step and stared around a landing with several closed doors. No way to know which one was right without taking a peek inside. It would be rude to do so, but the discussion taking place below was enough to tempt her. Clearly Rae and her mom needed a private moment or they would have followed her without delay. She tried to tune out of their whispered conversation but their words bounced up the hardwood stairs. Her only options were to listen or cover her ears. The latter just seemed silly.

Rae liked her. She knew that. But she had no idea what it meant for them. Now Rae, a woman Cori suspected was tight-lipped about her emotions, had told her mom. The fact seemed significant. Perhaps Norma's approval would encourage Rae to trust her emotions.

Cori pressed her fingers to her eyes, rubbing away the tired tension. What the hell was she doing in this house, about to delve into someone else's memories? She was on vacation. In Las Vegas. She was supposed to be gambling. Or drinking. Or relaxing by the pool. Not thinking about the wonderful possibility of a completely impossible relationship. Damn Rae and her sexy eyes and that cocky, flirty smile. Even as Cori cursed their meeting the first day, she felt herself go soft inside. Rae had entirely too much impact on her.

Tomorrow she had to climb on a plane and sit quietly while the pilot carried her away from the woman who constantly occupied her mind. A hard ache pulsed in Cori's chest. She refused to give it purchase but, still, it was there, underlying everything she thought, everything she did. She should end this foolishness now, for that's what it was, this self-torturing time spent with Rae. It would be over in—she glanced at her watch—less than twenty-four hours. There was no way she could carry hope beyond her time here. Rae was not the one-woman type.

And Cori didn't think she could settle for anything less.

The memory of that blond head clutched in Rae's hands loomed again, sending a surge of unwanted desire through her body. Cori shuddered and closed her mind off to the distracting image. Intellectually and emotionally, she didn't think she was willing to share Rae, but her body sure seemed willing to explore the possibilities. Fuck. That complicated things even further.

Footsteps sounded on the stairs, and a touch burned against the small of Cori's back. "What? You haven't finished yet?" Rae's voice was light and teasing.

"Not yet." Cori placed a careful, thankful kiss on Rae's cheek.

Effortlessly, Rae had chased the tension from her body. All the arguments in the world wouldn't convince her to spend the day anywhere but here. Not when Rae's palm felt so right against the small of her back and her breath made the hair on Cori's neck leap to attention.

"We're going in here." Rae opened a door on the left, revealing a dark room filled with boxes and furniture. Dust particles danced in the shaft of light filtering weakly through the sole time-darkened window.

"Tell me why we're doing this?" Cori asked.

Rae's fingers moved in lazy, unassuming circles, teasing her skin through the light cotton of her shirt. "Every year my mom gets this idea in her head that she should clear out all this junk. So, we spend a day up here with her memories, clean it out, and put most of the stuff back because she can't bear to part with any of it."

Cori examined her surroundings. A bucket of cleaning

supplies sat conspicuously in the middle of the dust and boxes. "Then I suppose we should get started."

Rae took her hand and kissed the fingers. "Be glad it's the storage room. Last week she had me dig up a busted pipe in her back yard. That was not fun."

"Okay, if we're going to do this some fresh air would help."

Rae released her and walked to the window. "It requires a little persuasion." She tapped the wooden sill gently with her palm and eased the window up. "There we go. Fresh air."

"That window's filthy." Cori selected a bottle of Windex and paper towels. "I'll clean it."

"Guess that leaves me with dusting." Rae armed herself with a can of Pledge and an old cloth.

Wiping the first layer of grime off the glass pane, Cori asked, "Do you spend every Sunday out here?"

She thought of her own family, her severe papa and meek mama, her myriad brothers and sisters. They avoided getting together unless there was no choice. Major holidays, weddings, her parents' anniversary. Even birthdays were spent with friends, not family. She couldn't imagine dedicating one day each week to doing chores around her parents' house. Her father's condemning glare was enough to drive her to drink. A fact that history had proven true more times than Cori cared to remember.

Rae shrugged. "Sundays belong to her."

"Hard to imagine."

Rae stiffened. "Why?"

Cori rushed to explain. She didn't know what upset Rae, but she wanted her reasons for saying that to be clear. "My family—well, my father, really—is a nightmare." She debated saying more, but decided against it. If Rae wanted to know, she'd ask.

"What about your mom?"

Such a simple question, but it pleased Cori no end. Even if nothing ever came of their connection, they were having the kind of conversation people had when they wanted to find out about each other. She tried to come up with a concise description of the woman who raised her.

"I don't know. It's like she's not really there. I have memories, just little snatches of her smiling at me, brushing my hair, teaching me to make tortillas. But then my father appears and she fades away into the shadows."

Rae's relationship with her mom was a stark contrast. They interacted with care and tenderness, even in the simplest things. That was obvious after just a few casual moments in the kitchen. Rae's mom was part of her life and knew who she was. Cori wasn't even certain if her mom knew what she did for a living or which side of town she lived on.

"I'm sorry." Rae's reflection greeted her in the window as she slid her arms around Cori's waist from behind. She rested her chin on Cori's shoulder.

Cori turned into her and kissed her waiting and willing lips. This kiss felt different than the ones they'd shared before. Cori had the impression that Rae was trying to heal her heart, long ago damaged by rough handling and neglect. Or maybe Cori just wanted to believe that was what motivated her. She wanted Rae to think of her as more than just a good fuck. Okay, an outstanding fuck, at least from Cori's point of view.

With a soft moan, Rae broke away. Her eyes were glazed and wanting. "My mom is going to come up here any minute now. Think she'll notice if I lock the door?"

"I'm willing to bet she'd notice," Norma said dryly from the top of the stairs.

Cori jumped backward, tripping over her own feet and thudding against the wall. She choked down the scrambling apologies of a teenager found fumbling on the sofa in the dark. Rae helped her catch her balance and gave her a chaste peck on the nose.

"Sorry, Mom." She winked at Norma. "Just couldn't control myself."

Cori went back to cleaning the window, mortified as Norma laughed easily along with her daughter. She couldn't fathom being so cavalier with a member of her own family about anything even remotely related to sex. They were barely tolerant of her being a lesbian and coped only providing she never brought up the subject. Yet here was Rae, clearly at ease, not embarrassed to have been caught in a compromising position. Thank God her mom had come up the stairs now, rather than later. Cori's clothes had a disturbing habit of falling off when Rae kissed her.

"Hey, Mom, remember this trip?" Rae sat on the trunk she'd been dusting, a photo album open in her lap.

Norma leaned over her shoulder, smiling. She gestured for Cori to join them. "That trip was horrible." Her laughter belied her statement as she fingered the edges of a faded snapshot of Rae lost in a giant pile of loose straw. "How old were you that year? Ten? Eleven?"

Rae's eyes were distant. "Ten, I think." She turned to Cori. "We were supposed to go to the coast. Mom had filled my head with pictures of the ocean. I was expecting warm water that went on forever. And sand castles and seashells."

Norma ruffled her hair. "Well, we made it halfway there. Damn car."

"The radiator sprung a leak. Not hard to fix, unless you're in the middle of nowhere. Which we were." Rae pointed at another picture. "We broke down just past a long dirt driveway. At ten it felt like we walked forever to get to their house. Looking back, I bet it wasn't more than a quarter of a mile."

"I felt so bad because I knew we wouldn't make it to the beach," Norma said. "But the second you saw those kids, your tired legs were forgotten. You were off like a shot."

Cori felt like a voyeur as she watched the exchange of memories between Rae and her mother. She wondered how many times they'd shared this ritual. Her heart swelled that she was included, even peripherally, in the special moment.

The rest of the afternoon passed too quickly, with the Sutherland women revisiting events of the past as they polished old medals, read newspaper clippings, and dusted mementos. Amazingly, this day would be the one Cori knew she'd remember most fondly from the whole trip. If her own mother saved similar trunks of memories, it was unbeknownst to her. The lack of physical reminders of their family's past was another sacrifice to her father's impatient will. There was never enough time to take a vacation. Never enough smiles to take a snapshot. Bittersweet sadness covered Cori like a blanket, and she wondered how she would ever be able board the plane and leave this behind.

CHAPTER TEN

Rae debated taking Cori back to her place, but Cori needed to pack. No amount of denial on her part would change that fact.

They were both strangely silent as Cori let them into her room. The easy comfort they'd enjoyed at her mom's was still there, but it was muted, painted over with the tense knowledge that this would be their last night together. Rae hoped she'd made the right choice by sharing the day with her mom rather than spending the time alone with Cori. She wished they could have one more day. With only a few hours between them and Cori's departure time, she wanted to hold Cori to her, not even getting out of bed, a rare, decadent treat she didn't afford herself, ever. That kind of leisure time didn't exist in her maxed schedule. Still, that's what she would have chosen with Cori. That's what she wanted now.

Her fingers trembled as she threw aside her own garments then unfastened Cori's buttons and slipped her blouse off her shoulders. She didn't try to hold back the rush of emotions that shivered through her body. In fact, she welcomed the feelings despite the new rawness they brought. She wanted Cori to know how deeply she was moved by her, that she couldn't see things the way she had. Something had changed.

Holding Cori's gaze, she undressed her, kneeling to remove her shoes, her socks, her pants. She ran her hands over Cori's body, up the tense lines of her calves, following the tremor over her thighs, around to caress the smooth, taut skin of her buttocks. She lingered on her knees, taking her time to explore the gentle swell of her tummy, the dip of her belly button, the indent at the base of her spine.

Cori moaned when her fingers glided up the inside of her thighs and she edged her legs slightly further apart. Rae kept her touch light, just the easy flow of her desire over Cori's flesh. Eventually, her movements were arrested by the sight of Cori, her head back and her lips parted slightly. Rae marveled. This woman, this *perfect* woman filled her with such a confusing mix of raw, undeniable hunger and tenderness she wanted to simultaneously fuck her so hard she'd forget her name and protect her from everything bad and hurtful in the world. She eased Cori back until her legs where against the bed. "Sit down, open yourself to me."

And Cori did. With her back arched and her long, satin-black hair fanned out on the comforter behind her, she opened her knees and squeezed and kneaded at her own breasts. "Please, Rae…"

What she'd ever done to deserve this kind of trust, Rae didn't know, but she thought she'd do anything to have the moment extend long enough to last a lifetime. She placed her hands high on the inside of Cori's knees, transfixed and half-afraid. "God, you're so beautiful."

She'd never said that to another woman. Not like that, like her beauty was the only truth she knew in her heart and if she didn't say the words, her body would burst with the burden of staying silent.

She smoothed her hands up the soft olive skin of Cori's inner thighs, then brushed dry, delicate kisses along the same path. When she reached the apex, she paused, steadying the quiver beneath her touch. Using her thumbs to gently pull back the hood, Rae revealed the glistening, tight bundle of nerves, and pressed a kiss lightly against the very tip.

Cori dropped back flat against the bed and twisted her fingers in Rae's hair. The insistent, sexy tug urged Rae closer. Cori lifted her hips and surged against her, openly begging for more. The unapologetic wantonness that had entranced Rae on their first night now held her captive completely. She wanted to plunge into her, spread her open, stretch her beyond full. Instead she stiffened her tongue and swiped it over Cori's pearl-hard clit, determined to go slow this time, to savor the burn.

Cori moved against her, rolling beneath the grip of her fingers. Rae dug in harder, overwhelmed by the urge to pin her down. Fearing that she might bruise the soft skin of Cori's thighs, she tried to relax her hold but she needed this too much to think beyond the slick, sweet slide of her tongue against Cori. She flexed her thumbs and they slipped dangerously close, almost sliding inside. Cori jerked up, urging her deeper. Rae eased away, moving her tongue with increased speed. She could feel Cori's body tightening, her orgasm gathering like a storm beneath the surface. Working her thumbs down Cori's crease, she pressed against her lower opening and lingered there, not pushing any further, pulsing in time to Cori's moans. She worked her clit harder, sucking it between her teeth, flicking her tongue, then flattening it smooth against the tip.

Cori bucked and thrashed through her orgasm, pulling away from Rae and curling in a tight, rocking ball on the bed. Rae climbed after her, gathering her close, back to front. She held her, smoothing her hands over her hair, whispering nonsense words of comfort in her ears, rocking with her, until the tide subsided and Cori returned to her.

"Oh, my God." Cori turned until they were pressed together, chest to chest. Her eyes were dazed. She didn't say anything more.

"You like?"

Normally, just knowing her partner had come was enough for Rae. She didn't need to discuss the details. With Cori, however, she wanted to know everything. She wanted to be certain that Cori would carry this memory with her, that she would picture Rae's face from this moment on, no matter who she was with. She wanted to be one Cori thought of as she came.

"Yes." Cori kissed Rae soundly. "I like."

Rae scooted up against the headboard and guided Cori into the crook of her arm. Cori had the best skin ever, the best body ever, too, for that matter. And it fit so deliciously next to hers.

"What do you want to do tonight?" Rae asked. "We haven't had dinner yet." It was presumptuous to assume ownership of Cori's time, the last night of her vacation, but she couldn't help it. She wasn't willing to give up even a moment in her company.

"I'm not feeling like getting dressed…ever again." Cori stretched across her and grabbed the menu from the nightstand. "How does room service sound?"

They decided to split a pizza, not the best choice from the menu, but food seemed unimportant. As they waited, content to simply hold each other and ignore the passing of time, Rae swore she could hear Cori purring against her, deep in her throat, like a big, satisfied, sexy as hell, naked kitty.

"There's this pizza place by my apartment called Jack-O's." She curled her fingers through Cori's hair. "They use all fresh ingredients. Instead of pre-shredded cheese out of a bag, they get their mozzarella in balls, covered in water, and they put it through this giant food processor type thing to shred it up. And the tomatoes are so fresh and plump, it's like they came out of someone's garden, straight to the pizza. You order the pizza and they toss the dough right then. Anytime you walk in there, you see these white, stretchy, wobbly Frisbees flying in the air. It's amazing."

"Sounds heavenly."

Rae could almost smell the ever present rosemary and sage that filled the air. "It is. We'll have to go some time."

Cori's smile didn't quite make it to her eyes. A knock sounded on the door and Rae slipped into a robe and retrieved their meal. They ate spread out over the bed. It wasn't nearly as good as Jack-O's, but she loved it anyway. Naked Cori made up for mediocre pizza any day.

"Tell me about your work." She knew very little about Cori's job, save the occupation.

"Well, I work for a full-service salon called Eden Body Works. Julie's there, too."

Rae had forgotten about Cori's friend. She glanced at the door, wondering when she would show up again. "Do you like massage therapy?"

Cori shrugged. "It's okay."

"Why aren't you a singer?" Rae knew enough about the music industry from Kel to know she sounded hopelessly naïve with that question, but Cori was talented. She could make a living at it if she wanted to.

"The market isn't the same in Seattle as it is here. The music industry is a big part of the city, but because there are more bands than gigs, the work tends to be low paying for most. There are a lot of very good, very out-of-work musicians and singers."

Of course it would be different away from Las Vegas. Sometimes Rae forgot how different her city's commerce base was from the rest of the country's.

"But you would if you could?" The question burned in Rae's lungs. If Cori lived in Vegas, a career change would be possible.

"Sure, who wouldn't? Every little girl dreams of being a rock star, doesn't she?"

Rae pictured a teenage Cori dancing around her room in her underwear, singing into a hairbrush. She smiled. "I suppose."

"At any rate, I'm not a rock star. I'm a hungry massage therapist." Cori helped herself to another slice of pizza. "What about you? You said you wanted the corner office. What does that mean in Vegas?"

The same thing it means the world over, Rae suspected. That she was a greedy, money-hungry, hell-bent on success ladder climber. "The big offices in Vegas are bigger than anywhere else." She smiled her best pirate-looking-for-treasure smile. "In a city based on sinful excesses, it's required."

For no reason that Rae could understand, Cori kissed her, just a quick press of her lips that told her she was happy in the moment.

"Right now I'm okay dealing blackjack," Rae continued. "I'm still in school and anything more would be hard to juggle. And I can only go so far without the degree, so it's the first priority."

"And then what?" Cori shifted the pizza tray to the night table and moved in closer. She didn't touch Rae beyond laying her palm easily against her thigh, but her nearness was soothing.

"Ultimately, I want my own property." Rae explained how

most resorts in Las Vegas were incorporated. In other parts of the country, hotels had managers. Here, the suit in charge was the CEO of a multi-million dollar company. "I want a car with a driver, a vacation home that I never use because I'm too busy—"

"Hah!" Cori interrupted. "I won't let you get away with that."

"No, I don't imagine you will." Rae was ridiculously pleased, forgetting for a moment what she'd been planning to say next. "I want a big house and a housekeeper to go with it, and a pool that stretches out into the desert."

Rae wondered if Cori would be comfortable in the house of her dreams and decided it didn't matter. She would be happy with whatever house Cori chose, her dream easily transferable to a new address. A hammer hit her chest then. Cori was leaving tomorrow. The room was suddenly too cold and Rae wanted more than the memory of a shared pizza to come home to after work.

"When do you leave?" She averted her eyes.

The words were soft, easily lost in the ever present hum of the air conditioner. If not for the movement of her lips, Cori would have thought that she'd imagined the question. Surely the tint of sadness in Rae's voice was more wishful thinking than real emotion. She cupped Rae's neck, letting her fingers play in the short hair on the back of her head. She wanted to forget the question, or at the very least, forget the answer, if only for the next few minutes. The tips of Rae's dark lashes, luscious and long without a trace of mascara, quivered as she leaned into Cori's touch.

Cori pressed her lips to Rae's and trailed her fingers over her skin, stopping at the inside curve of her waist. She was so vulnerable, her body exposed and inviting. The longer Cori went without answering, the heavier Rae's breathing became. A few more seconds and her eyes would close on the question, like the weight of the answer was too much to bear.

"I have to be at the airport by seven in the morning." Cori was surprised that the words had finally spilled out. She hadn't intended to speak. She didn't want the deadline hanging between them, coloring their last night together. She just wanted to curl up in Rae's arms and not think about life after Las Vegas.

"Can I take you to the airport?" Rae asked.

You can take me anywhere, Cori thought. "I'd like that."

Rae's eyes shimmered, the yearning stark on the surface. Her expression was guarded, yet vulnerable. "Will you come back?"

It wasn't an unreasonable question. Lots of people were frequent flyers when it came to Vegas. For Cori, though, this was a one-time trip. But she couldn't bring herself to say so. "I don't know."

Like a thundercloud casting a shadow on a sunny day, Rae's expression darkened. She parted her lips and paused mid-breath, the exhalation trapped by her obvious desire to say something more. Cori waited, hope blossoming. She almost begged Rae to speak, ask the question she desperately wanted to hear. It would be so simple. One word, that's all she needed. *Stay...* But it never came.

Rae drew her close and Cori melted into her, the length of her body pressed against Rae's. One arm was draped over her waist, Rae's palm flat against Cori's back. Rae gripped her shoulder with the other hand, squeezing tight, almost crushing. Then Cori felt the pressure ease and Rae's touch turned to a light easy caress, her fingers moving to the pulse point behind her ear, into the hair at the base of her neck and around again.

She kissed Cori with the same gentle exploration, a sensual brush of her lips, lingering, exploring. Cori felt as though Rae was worshipping her, memorizing the inside of her mouth.

Cori opened herself, inviting Rae deeper. This kiss, the languid slide of Rae's tongue inside her mouth, would be the moment she would remember. The last four days had been an emotional and sexual roller-coaster, with Rae at the control panel. She'd taken her higher, dropped her lower, and crashed through her with an intensity that would leave an indelible mark. But this moment, this gentle lull that stretched and flowed, this would stay sharp in Cori's mind.

Cori stopped at the security checkpoint. She should have said good-bye at the drop-off area, but she couldn't bring herself to let go. Rae's hand felt natural in hers, like they were born to hold hands.

"I have to go," she said. The thought of crossing through the gates felt like a prison sentence. Her life, her family, waited for her in Seattle, and all she wanted was to curl up in bed with Rae and never leave.

"I know." Rae's voice was resolute, but Cori detected an underlying current of hurt.

She squeezed Rae's hand a little tighter. The plane was leaving in thirty-three minutes. She needed to hustle through security now if she was going to make it down the concourse in time. Maybe they wouldn't notice if she sneaked Rae onto the plane in her overnight bag.

"You have my number, right?" Cori knew she did, but she couldn't keep from asking again.

Rae kissed her fingers. "And you have mine."

"I really have to go."

"And I really don't want to you to," Rae said as though teasing, but her voice was husky with emotion.

Cori wanted to kiss her but held herself back. If she started, she wouldn't be able to stop until she kissed away every sad nuance.

"You'll call me?" Rae asked.

The pleading tone made it impossible for Cori to walk away. She tightened her grip on Rae's hand. "Yes."

"And I'll call you." Rae didn't sound convinced, like she knew that when Cori boarded the plane she'd be leaving her life forever.

Cori wanted to make promises, but she couldn't. Broken promises were far worse than no promises at all. Still, she wanted to find the magic words to erase the desperate longing that clouded Rae's face. She kissed her on the cheek, squeezed her fingers one last time, and gave herself over to the tide of departing passengers. She wished she'd met Rae in the days before increased security stopped visitors from venturing too far in the terminals. As soon as she was through the X-ray and metal detectors, she turned to wave good-bye one last time before resuming her journey.

Rae stood riveted in place as airport traffic moved around her. She appeared oblivious to the jostling bumps of other travelers as she stared after Cori. She raised her hand in a taut wave and the next time Cori glanced back, all she saw was Rae's back as she rounded the corner on the way out of the airport.

Her brain told her it was for the best. A weekend liaison under the neon lights of Las Vegas, wasn't that every tourist's dream? Her heart screamed at her to run out of the airport and into Rae's life. She couldn't let herself do that. If Rae had truly wanted her to stay, she would have asked. Cori wondered how long the sinking feeling in the pit of her stomach would haunt her. She knew Rae could chase away her longing with a touch, but until Rae held her again, it would stay with her like an unwanted visitor. Cori tried to shake off her melancholy as she plodded to the gate and boarded the plane. The fairytale was over. Time to get back to reality.

CHAPTER ELEVEN

Cori sat in her parents' driveway, the windshield wipers droning across the glass. Each time her view was cleared the relentless downpour obscured it immediately. She missed the warmth of the desert, the warmth of Rae's smile. She'd only been home a couple of days, but she was desperate to feel even a smidgen of what she'd felt with Rae.

Her mom had peeked around the curtain several times in the last fifteen minutes, but she hadn't come out. It was possible that she didn't recognize the light blue Toyota. Cori had only owned it for a few months and hadn't visited her parents since purchasing it. She needed to get in the house before her mom called the police. Or worse, her father.

Since her return from Las Vegas, the urge to visit her mom had pressed heavily on her, pushing her to make the trip across town. She'd put it off until tonight, knowing that Wednesday was her father's regular poker night. He never missed the game, claiming it gave him access to potential clients. Cori didn't understand how that was possible, as he'd played with the same five guys for as long as she could remember, but she wasn't about to point that out.

Now that she was here, confronted by the squat Portland-style house she'd grown up in, she started rethinking her decision to visit. It was not like she would walk through the door and discover that her mother had suddenly morphed into Norma Sutherland. Still, it was too late to simply put her car in reverse and pretend she'd never been here. Too bad.

Cori turned off the engine, pulled her jacket tight against the rain, and opened the door. When she rang the doorbell she heard rustling footsteps followed by an unnatural silence. It would be just her luck to have her mom pretend she wasn't home while she huddled on the doorstep in the rain.

Cori pounded on the door. "Mami, let me in, *por favor.* It's cold out here."

Slowly, the door opened an inch, chain still in place, and her mother peered cautiously through the crack.

"*Dios mío!*" She slammed the door and a moment later, threw it open all the way. "Corina, come inside. Why were you lurking in your car like a psychopath? You scared me to death. That car. Is it new?"

The familiar scolding and pseudo ease faded as her mother led her down the long hall to the formal living room, a place for guests, rather than to the kitchen table. Family portraits, with their fake smiles and stiff poses, lined the walls, demarcating the passing years of her childhood. The last one was taken the Christmas before her youngest brother graduated high school. In the years since, the whole family had never come together for the holidays. Her mother and father, Louisa and Joaquin "Call me Henry, we're in America now" Romero, sat ramrod straight in the middle of the picture Cori stared at, chastely holding hands, their children standing in a semicircle around them. Nobody looked happy.

"What were you doing out there?" Louisa sat on the edge of the couch, folding and unfolding her hands in her lap. A large portrait of Cori's late grandfather dominated the room from its position of honor over the fireplace. "I almost called your father."

"I'm sorry, Mami. I didn't mean to scare you." Cori gave a mental sigh of relief. She'd come inside just in time. "I'm glad you didn't disturb Papi."

"Is that a new car?" her mother repeated. In her usual fashion, Louisa left the real questions unasked, preferring to stay with safe topics.

"I bought it a few months ago." Cori shifted self-consciously. The furniture in this room was for show, not comfort. Rain water pooled on the hardwood floor at her feet. "It's a Toyota."

"Oh, that's nice." Louisa glanced at the clock on the wall. "Do you like it?"

"It gets good gas mileage." Cori wondered how many times she'd have to stop for fuel if she left for Vegas right now. Three, maybe four? "Do you want to go for a ride?"

"No, no, no." Louisa shook her head briskly. "Your father will be home soon. I don't want him to worry."

Cori's phone vibrated in her pocket, silent to her mother, but offering her a much needed escape from the thick tension of the room. She let it go to voice mail.

"How is Papi?"

"He is good. You know your father, he works too much."

For the first time, Cori listened beyond her mother's words. *He works too much* was Louisa's standard answer to any question about Joaquin. She looked tired. Maybe she was tired of cooking and cleaning for a man who was never home, a man who never said thank you. A man who had driven all of her children away, one after the other. Forget "tired." Her mother looked lonely.

"How are *you*, Mami?"

Louisa stiffened. "I'm fine." She said it with finality. No room for further discussion.

Cori heard a door open and close, and then her father's voice. "Louisa? There's a car in the driveway. Who's here?" He stopped short in the entry to the family room when he saw Cori. "Corina."

He held out his hands. Even without the love, he expected his children to greet him with an arm's-length hug and kiss on the cheek. Cori complied.

"Papi, you look well."

Joaquin was a tightly built man. His body, his clothes, his hair, even his precise mustache, were all crisp, with sharp edges and hard lines. While he would never be accused of being inviting, he was almost always described as compelling.

He evaluated Cori, his dark eyes seeking out every imperfection. "Corina, have you gained weight?"

"No, Papi." She'd actually lost a few pounds since she'd last seen him, but he would never acknowledge that.

"Are you sure?" He tipped his head, his finger and thumb stroking the sides of his mustache. "Well, no matter." He sat next to Louisa, his arms stretched across the back of the couch.

"Your game ended early?" Cori asked as she sat carefully in the same damp spot.

"Yes." Joaquin offered no further explanation. He rarely did. "Tell me, Corina, have you met a nice boy yet?"

Cori smiled, her teeth clenched, lips stretched thin. "No, Papi. You know I haven't."

"Oh, that's right. Boys aren't good enough." He looked at his wife. "What's she call herself, Mami? A lesbian?" He drew the word out, over enunciating every syllable.

Cori stood. "It's time for me to go."

His lips thinned. "Sit down, Corina." It wasn't an invitation.

Cori hesitated, cursing herself for ever coming here, then sat. "Yes, Papi."

"We so rarely see you. What have you been doing with yourself?"

No matter how many times she'd been on the receiving end, it never ceased to amaze her how easily her father could turn a polite question into a judgment and inquisition all at once.

"I went to Las Vegas last week. Learned how to play blackjack." She hoped that turning the conversation to gambling would distract her father from criticizing her.

"Really? I haven't been to Vegas in years. Not since you were little." He leaned forward, elbows on his knees. "Did you like it?"

Cori fleetingly thought of telling him about her trip, the parts she really liked, but doubted he wanted to know about Rae and her magic tongue. "Blackjack is kind of fun. I had a good teacher." Cori mentally smacked herself. Why did she say that?

"Good teacher?"

"One of the dealers taught me the rules." She kept her answer brief, hoping he would let the topic die. She glanced at the clock. A few more minutes and she'd be allowed to leave. She just had to bide her time without antagonizing him further. She glanced at her mother. Louisa sat tight-lipped, staring straight ahead.

"Did you do anything else while you were there?" he asked.

"I auditioned for a band."

"What?" her father barked, his laughter like machine-gun fire.

Cori didn't repeat herself. He'd heard her the first time and she already regretted saying it. No reason to give him further ammunition.

"Corina, you can't be serious?" He shook his head, the cruel smile fading. "And did you get the job?" His tone assured her that there was no possibility of that happening.

"I haven't heard back yet."

"It doesn't matter. You can't live in Las Vegas anyway." He waved his hand dismissively.

"Why not?" Cori tried to rein in her temper, hoping the question sounded curious rather than defiant.

Her father's eyes narrowed. "Because your family is here."

In the past, that answer would have been enough. But after seeing Rae and Norma, it meant very little, possibly nothing at all. Her parents weren't interested in sharing a loving relationship with their children. Her father simply wanted her around in case he needed her. Large, happy families impressed potential clients, he believed.

Cori bit back her answer. This was not the time to make a grand stand. There was no reason to even have the conversation. She'd heard from Rae once, via e-mail, and Kel hadn't contacted her at all. Nothing in Vegas was calling her there, so why argue the point?

"Yes, Papi."

Her father relaxed, settling back into his customary position, arms spread wide, left ankle resting on his right knee. "Good." He looked pointedly at the clock. "It's getting late. Your mother needs her rest."

Cori stood, relief washing through her. Parole had come earlier than expected. "I'm sorry to keep you."

She kissed her parents good-bye, let herself out the front door, and didn't stop until she was safely inside her car. She wanted to punch the steering wheel, scream to heaven, curse her father for every thoughtless word he ever spoke. Instead, she started the car and drove away, dialing up her voice mail as she went. The caller ID showed a number she didn't recognize with a Las Vegas area code. Maybe Rae had called while on a break at work.

Kel's voice greeted her. "Cori, sorry it took so long to get back to you. We discussed your audition and we all think that you'd make a good addition to our band. Call me so we can discuss the details."

Cori's hands shook as she pulled to the side of the road. Now she understood why talking on cell phones while driving was illegal in the state of Washington. She'd thought the law irrelevant, the product of legislators trying to avoid real issues like the rising cost of health care, but the message from Kel had her thoroughly distracted. Driving was the last thing on her mind.

Should she call her back? What would she say? Did she want to move? She was no longer dealing in abstracts. The offer was real. Las Vegas didn't have to be just a fond memory. Cori thought about her life in Seattle. She had her work, which had long since lost its luster, a family that she never saw, and a handful of friends. The only true constant in her life was the rain, and she'd gladly surrender that relationship.

What did Vegas have to offer? A career she'd dreamt about since she was a child. And Rae. Rae with her sun-bleached bangs dragging over Cori's skin as she kissed her way down her body. Rae with the devil-glint in her eyes and the too sexy *I know you want it* smile. Rae with her soft lips and the security Cori found only in her arms.

Rae.

Cori dialed Kel's number and prayed for voice mail. She didn't get her wish. She thanked Kel for calling, careful to say how flattered she was, how she was seriously considering the offer.

"What are you saying, Cori? You going to rock with us or what?" Kel's voice clearly said she couldn't imagine any answer other than *Yes!*

"I'm saying this is a big decision, relocating my life. Can I have a couple of days to think it over?"

"Why did you audition if you weren't sure?" Kel moved to full-on annoyed.

"I didn't think I had a chance." Cori left out the part about being more than a little drunk. "It was a 'what the hell, why not try?' moment. I didn't think anything would come of it."

"I can see that." Kel's voice softened. "You have until Saturday."

Cori thanked her again and ended the call. A decision like this needed to be made with a clear head. Would she even be considering it if Rae wasn't a potential part of the package? Cori stared at her cell phone. She wanted to call Rae and discuss what the move would mean to their relationship.

Did they even have a relationship?

No, they didn't. She needed to decide what she wanted without Rae. She dropped the cell phone in the passenger seat and resumed her journey home. Maybe after a long, hot bath, the answer would come to her.

CHAPTER TWELVE

Rae pushed her hair out of her eyes and took a long drag of her dwindling Camel. The dull throb of Nirvana pushed through the window, reminding her of the party in progress around her. She flicked her cigarette into the gutter, tempted to call it an early night and just head home. Kel would understand.

"What are you doing out here?" Kel held out a fresh longneck Bud. "The party's inside."

Rae took the drink. Early night or not, it would be a shame to let a cold beer go to waste. "I'm just catching some air."

Kel nodded and scuffed her worn motorcycle boots against the curb. "We can go if you want."

Rae shook her head. She tapped out two cigarettes, lit them, and passed one to Kel. She never left a party early. And *never* alone. Kel, hot little boi that she was, wasn't the type of woman Rae had a reputation for seducing. They both looked for other playmates. Partying with Kel this early on a Friday night was unheard of. The band typically didn't finish work until four in the morning, sometimes later.

"How long until you're back at work?" Rae asked.

"We still have to replace Nikki."

"Auditions were last week. Why the delay?"

"We made an offer."

Rae's heart thudded in her chest and she forced herself to speak slowly. "Is it anybody I know?"

"Yeah, your *friend* Cori, the one from Seattle."

Rae smiled. "Cori?" Hell, even her voice was smiling. The more she tried to control it, the more she smiled.

"I take it that's a good thing."

Rae nodded. "When does she start?"

"Don't know." Kel shrugged. "She asked for a few days to decide."

Rae's heart fell. She'd heard from Cori yesterday with no mention of Kel's offer. Now she knew why. Cori wasn't going to take it. "When will you know for sure?"

"I'll call her some time next week."

Rae crushed her half-smoked Camel under her heel. "Let's go in."

"Right on." Kel threw her arm around Rae's shoulder. "Sharon Gambini is here with her new girlfriend. She's looking for you."

Rae raised an eyebrow. "Really?"

Sharon Gambini was a true Vegas party girl. She burned through girlfriends in less time than it took Rae to smoke a carton. The revolving door to her heart was due in large part to the revolving door to her bedroom. Sharon loved the security of having a girlfriend, but wasn't willing to give up her roving affections. There was only one reason she looked for people at parties and it wasn't to trade recipes.

"Really." Kel led her through the front door. "And you should let her put a smile back on your face."

Rae flipped her hair back and tried for a wicked, devious grin. "Maybe I'll put a smile on hers."

"That's the spirit." Kel nodded toward a rapidly approaching Sharon. "Sharon, I found Rae for you."

Sharon ran her hand down Rae's arm. "It's good to see you," she purred, sex dripping from the words. "Have you met Dar?" She gestured to her companion, a woman with glaring eyes and a possessive arm around Sharon's waist.

"It's nice to meet you." Rae offered a hand. Sharon traced the lines of the grass-skirt-wearing hula girl on Rae's shirt as she shook hands with Dar. "Are you new to Vegas?"

"Been here a few weeks." Dar flexed her jaw, grinding her teeth as she watched Sharon.

Rae considered her options. Sharon was a sure thing, fun in bed with no complicated morning after. Dar, however, looked like she wanted to kick her ass. Not a very appealing prospect. Still, the couple offered a needed distraction from her thoughts of Cori. Time to divide and conquer.

"Sharon, do you need a fresh drink?"

Dar glared.

Sharon smiled. "Yes, Rae, I do."

She placed extra emphasis on each word, making her sound like a damsel in distress to Rae's knight on a horse. Rae never realized how supremely annoying her voice was until tonight.

"Wait here." Rae backed her up against a wall and kissed her low on the neck. "Dar and I will be right back." She grabbed Dar's arm. "Come on, Dar."

"What?" Dar looked at Sharon. "We both don't need to go."

They were in the kitchen before Dar got the protest out completely. Rae plucked a wine cooler from a bucket of ice and handed it to her. "You like Sharon?"

"Yeah." Dar nodded slowly.

"Then stop acting like a jealous gorilla. The only way she'll keep you is if you take her as is." It was unsolicited advice and dangerous to boot. Rae waited to see how it would be received.

"What do you mean?" Dar chewed her fingernail.

"You're going to drive her away. She needs room to play."

Dar flared. "But she wants to play with you."

"No." Rae again debated calling it an early night. This sure thing was proving to be a lot of work. "She wants to play with us."

Realization spread over Dar's face. "Really? And that's okay with you?"

Dar, with her shaved head, low-riding board shorts, and too-big T-shirt, wasn't the type that Rae would generally pursue. But for every hard edge on Dar, Sharon had two soft curves to make up for it. Rae was ready to spend a few hours exploring the differences. Most importantly, neither of them was short, dark, and fiery.

"Yeah, but I think a better question would be is it okay with *you*? She's your girlfriend."

Dar nodded and headed to the next room like a woman with a mission. She turned once to make sure Rae followed.

Sharon winked at Rae as she kissed Dar to say thank you for the wine cooler. "Did you two work out your differences?" she asked.

In answer, Rae held Sharon's gaze and kissed Dar. She lingered a moment, drawn in by the taste of good ale and spearmint.

"I guess you did."

Rae traded Dar's beer and gum for the sugary sweet residue of wine cooler on Sharon's tongue.

"Let's go upstairs," Sharon said.

Rae followed them up the stairs, aware of the empty blank in her groin where fire should have been sparking. She held out hope that this encounter would wake up her slumbering libido. So far nothing had shaken her out of the Cori-induced funk she was stranded in.

The first room they tried was occupied, as was the second. Dar, her own shirt off and tucked in her back pocket, had worked her way through the buttons on Sharon's shirt and was trying to remove her panties without taking off her skirt. The look on her face said they'd crossed the point of no return as she tried the next door. Thankfully the room was empty or Rae was sure they would have ended up on the floor in the hall.

Dar led them into the dimly lit space, Rae by the hand, Sharon by the lips. Rae pulled Sharon between them and kissed the back of her neck where the collar had fallen away. Her shirt hung loose, open in the front, and Rae wanted to trace the lace edge of her bra with her tongue. She squeezed Sharon's breasts, pinching the nipples between her fingers as she bit down hard on her shoulder. Dar groaned, her eyes glazed with desire. She ground her pelvis against Sharon, driving her closer to Rae.

Rae slid her hands lower, watching to make sure Dar was still into sharing. A flare-up of jealousy at this point could prove painful for everyone involved. They were too connected with teeth and flesh not to be cautious.

"Watch," she said to Dar as she inched Sharon's skirt up until it was bunched around her waist.

With Sharon's panties already off, Rae had unfettered access to her perfect shaved pussy. She urged Sharon to widen her stance, spreading herself open, then smoothed her hands along the soft skin on the inside of her thighs. Sharon tilted her head back, resting it on Rae's shoulder, eyes closed. She gripped Rae's hands, coaxing her closer to her center.

"You always know what I like," she breathed.

Rae pulled Sharon's lips apart, her thumb beating a steady pattern on her clit. She kept her eyes on Dar. "On your knees."

"Yesss," Sharon hissed as Dar hit the floor.

Rae braced herself against the door and shifted her position lower. She knew from experience that Sharon came hard and loud. She didn't want to drop her.

The wet, hot slick of Dar's tongue pushed against Rae's fingers, tugging a small flicker of interest from her. She should have been blazing, but mostly she wanted Sharon to hurry. She surrendered her hold to Dar's mouth and brought one hand up to Sharon's breast. She pulled and tweaked the nipple, twisting it through the lace. The other hand she placed on the top of Dar's head. The stubble prick of her hair pebbled against Rae's palm as she held the younger woman tight to Sharon.

Sharon rocked against Dar's mouth and her body drew tight. Rae exhaled in her ear, the hot breath bringing bumps to the surrounding skin. "You are so fucking hot, spread out with Dar's tongue inside you, fucking you." The words sounded hollow to Rae, but Sharon quaked in her arms. "That's it. Let it go." Rae kept talking. "I've got you. Dar's on her knees, licking your hard clit, begging you to come in her mouth."

Rae held Sharon's earlobe between her teeth, biting down slightly between the words. Sharon rocked back, her body rigid. Just a little more and she'd be over the edge and Rae could go home.

Dar worked her right hand into her own shorts. Her low, humming moans filled the room.

Rae urged, "Do you hear her? She's touching herself, fucking herself as she sucks you off. Come for her, Sharon. Come for her now."

Sharon screamed, her body vibrating as she doubled over, pulling Rae with her. A moment later, Dar growled and fell limp to the floor, her hand motionless in her shorts. Rae held Sharon for a moment longer then straightened. She needed out of the room, out of the house, out of her skin. A shower wouldn't wash this away. She needed Cori.

Sharon's voice, confused and concerned, followed Rae down the stairs. Halfway to her car she got her cell phone out and dialed Cori's number. Five rings and then voice mail. Where was she? It was Friday night. Was she out with friends? Did she have a date? Was she doing the same thing Rae just did?

Rae's stomach rolled. "Cori, it's Rae. Call me." She forced herself to breathe. "I just...I just need to hear your voice. Please. Call me."

Cori was ready to let Las Vegas go. It would be foolhardy, a child's dream, to rearrange her life, drop everything, and run off to a city fueled by neon sin. She should call Kel and tell her that although she was flattered, she wouldn't be able to join the band. She sat, fingers midair over the keys, trying to convince her heart that she needed to heed the logic of her head. Still, she couldn't bring herself to dial.

The answer had come to her earlier that night, rising in clarity as she neared the bottom of a bottle of self-pity. The hours passed, along with the alcohol from her system, and the desperation of Rae's phone message sank in. Cori needed to hear her voice, too. How could she deny the plea?

Still not quite sober, she dialed.

"Hello." Rae's voice was gravel rough. A product of sleep? Or cigarettes? "Cori?"

"Hi, Rae."

Since Cori's departure, they'd limited their communications to e-mail, a few stilted and polite lines filled with the happenings of the day. Now the burning ache to be with Rae rose with each breath coming through the phone line.

"I miss you," Rae said.

Cori wondered at the immediate confession. Out of character and too revealing. What did it mean? "I miss you, too."

"Where were you tonight? When I called." Rae hesitated. "I didn't disturb you, did I?"

"I was here."

"Oh."

Silence, like a brick-and-mortar wall loomed between them.

"Maybe I shouldn't have called," Rae said.

"Why did you?"

"I...like I said, I miss you."

"What made you think of me?" Did she haunt Rae's thoughts the way Rae haunted hers?

"I was at a party."

Cori thought of *that* party again. "What did you do at the party?"

The question was out before she realized it. Why did she care? She wasn't there to police Rae's orgasms and claim them for her own. But still she wanted them, each and every one. If Rae's breath hitched, if her heart pounded, if her clit exploded, Cori wanted to own every last beat.

"Was it like last time, when I saw you?" she asked.

"Yes." Barely a whisper.

"Tell me."

It didn't matter that they should be talking about Kel's offer, the band, the possibility of Cori's moving, or what waited for her if she did. All she needed was Rae's confession.

"I thought about leaving. It was too loud, too smoke-filled, too crowded."

Rae's reasoning didn't ring true. She worked in that exact environment every night and loved it. There had to be more to her wanting to leave than she was sharing.

"Go on," Cori prompted.

"Then I ran into..." A long pause, then a cautious, "Do you want to know her name?"

The careful consideration, a lesson learned, touched Cori. "Yes, tell me."

"Sharon. She was there with her girlfriend, Dar."

"Describe them."

"Dar has a shaved head. Sharon is tall. Fake California tan. Long blond hair. Tiny waist and perfect gravity-defying tits."

Probably also fake. "Did you touch them?" Cori asked.

"Yes."

"What did her girlfriend do?"

"Watched."

"Tell me."

"We found a room, the three of us, and barely made it inside. Dar half stripped on the way up the stairs. She had Sharon's shirt open and her panties off before I could close the door behind us."

Cori laid back, her head on the arm of her couch, and pulled her T-shirt up. Her nipples were hard.

"Sharon had on a black lace bra," Rae said. "I wanted to bite my way through it, but I was behind her, kissing her neck. I squeezed and pinched her nipples. The lace was soft."

"Did she like it?" Cori pictured Rae's fingers working her own nipples to straining attention. "Did you like it?"

"She moaned." Rae's breathing accelerated. "I like your

breasts better. They're soft and real. I wish I was there now with my mouth on you. I'd suck you until you screamed."

"Did you kiss her?"

"Yes." Rae groaned. "Fuck-me red lipstick. I smeared it. Her lips tasted sweet from too much wine. I prefer yours. Yours are luscious. I could kiss you all day and taste your breath and never get enough."

"Did you fuck her?" God, Cori didn't *want* to know the answer but she *needed* to. She squeezed her breasts, rolling the nipples between her thumb and fore finger. "Was she wet?"

"Dripping. But I didn't fuck her. I wanted you, not her."

Cori growled. The memory of Rae watching her the first night in Vegas was hot in her mind, urging her hands lower. She could feel Rae's breath on her thighs as she breathed her in. The desperation. "Did you leave her wanting?"

"I held her open and stroked her clit while Dar tongue-fucked her."

"Oh, God."

"I was behind her. Sucking her throat...biting her ear... talking to her. And her girlfriend was on her knees, knuckle-deep inside her, licking her clit and jerking herself off at the same time."

Cori worked her clit, flicking her fingers over it with driving relentless rhythm. Rae's voice and her own knowing touch had brought her dangerously close to climax. "What did you say?"

"I don't remember. I wanted you, my hands on you, your tongue in my mouth, your sweat on my skin."

"Are you touching yourself?"

"Yes."

"Did you come with her?"

Rae's answer came swiftly. "No."

"Why not?"

"She wasn't you."

"Are you coming now?"

"Yes," Rae gasped.

Cori exploded. Rae's soft groans matched her own. The color in the room seeped to black, then swirled into focus in a hail of pinpoint light. Rae's ragged breathing held Cori, their only connection through the phone.

"How do you do that?" Rae sounded spent.

Cori laughed, proud of herself. "You're easy."

"Pleased with yourself, aren't you?"

Cori was. Earlier that night, Rae had been alone with two willing women. They couldn't make her come like Cori could with only a few words, some shared memories, and several hundred miles between them. Sadness filtered in, replacing the warm afterglow. Was this what life with Rae would be like if they tried to be together in Las Vegas? Rae's transgression followed by confession? Was Rae capable of commitment and exclusivity? Or would Cori be resigning herself to a life of better-than-what's-her-name fucks? That wasn't good enough.

"Cori, I really miss you," Rae's voice was hoarse.

It seemed the only thing left to say between them.

"I know, Rae. I miss you, too."

Cori ended the call without a promise to speak again. She couldn't continue like this, barely recovering only to tear the scab off and open herself to the loss all over again.

CHAPTER THIRTEEN

Cori choked down a handful of aspirin, her answer to the thrumming in her head. God knows, she deserved the killer headache but that didn't mean she had to embrace it. A simple glass of water before she fell asleep would have held it at bay, preventing the alcohol from dehydrating her body. But rather than getting up after talking to Rae, she'd lain there until she fell asleep. Her body throbbed with a satisfying after-orgasm hum, but her heart ached with loss.

This was ridiculous. Rae couldn't give her what she wanted. Even if she did accept the gig and move to Las Vegas, Rae wouldn't stop being a party-hard playgirl. That would never be enough to satisfy Cori. She needed to move on. Her cell phone blinked at her. Someone had left another voice mail while she was on the phone with Rae and too busy to switch over. Cori wanted to crawl back in bed and hide from the day. Instead she pushed the button to collect her message.

"Cor, it's Julie. If you don't call me soon, I'm going to assume you've been kidnapped by aliens and report it to the *National Enquirer.* Seriously. Call me."

Cori dialed and held the phone a few inches from her ear. The grating ringing noise hurt her sound-sensitive head.

"You're alive." Julie greeted her far too cheerfully.

Cori pressed her fingers to her temple. "Easy does it. I've got a thumping headache."

"That'll do. What are you doing tonight?"

Cori had planned to stay in, call it an early night, and catch up on reading and sleeping. Not necessarily in that order. "Nothing much."

"Come out with me on a double date."

Cori groaned. "No, I hate blind dates."

"I know, but I've dated Lisa a few times and met her friend Gretchen. She's nice. Totally your type. It'll be fun."

Julie's version of totally Cori's type meant single and breathing. To her, any available lesbian was a good one. It didn't matter if she was psycho-stalker crazy woman known to have U-Haul on speed dial. In fact, the trait rated higher on Julie's scorecard than commitment-phobic players like Rae.

"Come on, Cori." Julie's voice bordered on whiny. "It's a low-pressure evening. Dinner, that's it. Maybe karaoke afterward. Please."

"Julie…"

"You can't say no. Lisa already told Gretchen you'll be there."

"Fuck."

Cori thought about hanging up. Fuck Lisa, a woman she didn't know. And fuck her unsponsored promise to Gretchen, a woman she didn't want to know. But if she stayed in tonight, she was destined for a repeat of last night. Too much rum and Rae talking her through a shattering orgasm. Wallowing wouldn't help her get over it. She needed a distraction from the fairytale and Julie was offering a night out.

"Is that a yes?" Julie pressed.

"Yes, all right. Fine. What time?"

❖

The doorbell sounded as Cori ran the brush through her hair one last time. The light sundress she'd chosen would not be enough to fight off the cool April air, but her heart, which was still in the desert, wouldn't let her choose another outfit. She settled a sweater around her shoulders and answered the door with a forced smile.

A woman with short, sandy brown hair held out a bouquet of white daisies wrapped in crinkly red paper. "Hi, you must be Cori." She grinned, dimples and all. "I'm Gretchen."

"Thanks." Cori took the flowers and invited her in. "Let me just put these in water then we can go."

"Cool. Julie said you like flowers. I hope these are okay."

"They're beautiful." Just not from Rae. And not tulips and lilies. Perhaps that was a good thing. Daisies sent a different message: *Keep it simple.* "It was very sweet of you to think of it."

"No problem." Gretchen pushed her hands into the pockets of her baggy Levi's while she waited.

Cori moved the flowers to a vase with minimum fuss, not taking the time to trim the stems or arrange the blossoms. The niceties could wait until later, when she didn't have a North Face–wearing, outdoorsy dyke watching from her living room.

"That's it. We can go." She ushered Gretchen out, pausing briefly to lock the deadbolt. "What's on the agenda?"

"Dinner at The Wildrose. We'll see from there."

The suggestion in Gretchen's voice was not lost on Cori. It was clear that, in the brief minutes they'd known each other, Gretchen had decided sex was on the menu if Cori was interested. Cori stiffened when Gretchen's hand landed gently on her back as they made their way to the car.

The drive to The Wildrose was short and quiet. Cori was

grateful. Small talk with Julie was one thing, but she wasn't up for playing nice with strangers. What had she been thinking when she agreed to come out tonight? She made sure she walked a few steps away from her "date" as they approached the familiar venue.

"Have you been here before?" Gretchen asked as she held the door for Cori.

"Of course." Every dyke in Seattle had been to the Rose.

"I love this place." Gretchen offered a devilish smile that only made Cori miss Rae more.

"Yeah," Julie chimed in from among the women gathered just inside the entrance. "The food is awesome and the service is great."

She wasn't wrong about the service. It was still early on Saturday night and before the door closed behind them, a menu-carrying hostess greeted them and led them to an open table in the corner. It was secluded with taper candles providing the limited light. Cori ordered rum with ice and a dash of lime. She needed all the help she could get to loosen up and make it through the night. A fruity umbrella drink just wouldn't cut it.

"Straight rum?" Julie nudged her. "Rough week?"

Cori shrugged. "I saw my parents on Wednesday. Still trying to recover."

Gretchen squeezed her knee. "That does it for me every time."

The restaurant offered a simple menu, with smoked ham and mac, a popular favorite according to the waiter. Cori craved pizza with fresh basil and rosemary, dough tossed new for every order. She smiled, agreed to the pasta, and asked for another rum. The first one would be gone all too soon.

The conversation stalled uncomfortably between placing the order and dinner arriving.

After several minutes of silent contemplation of her lime

wedge, Cori asked, "So, Gretchen, what do you do? Julie didn't say." She might as well try to have a good time.

"I own Hike N Dyke. You ever hear of it?"

With the exception of one memorable visit to the Hoover Dam, Cori was not much for the outdoors. "No, what do you do there?"

"Sell hiking and camping gear, as well as coordinate lesbian-only camping trips. You should come some time."

"Yeah, it's a blast." Lisa kissed Julie. "You'd like it, hon. Making love under the stars."

Thankfully, the waiter arrived with their food so Cori didn't have to hear Julie's views on sex in the wilderness.

"Remember what happened last time?" Gretchen smiled.

For the first time her face was filled with genuine happiness instead of the polite lesbian-on-the-make grins Cori had witnessed so far. She could be friends with someone with a smile like that. She swirled her rum, tuning out the conversation around her. Once lesbians got talking about wilderness adventures, the anecdotes never stopped coming. She didn't really care what happened when the skunk wandered through camp, sending everyone into a panic.

One hour, a plate of cheesy pasta, and three rums later, dinner was blissfully over. Gretchen's stories—each including at least one reference to her dog, a tent, and a pair of hiking shoes—appeared to be winding down. Still, Cori was caught off guard when Gretchen asked what she did for a living.

All eyes were on her and she thought hard about her uncertain future. "Oh, I'm a massage therapist. I work with Julie."

Gretchen looked pointedly at her hands. "So, you know how to use your fingers?"

Cori barely kept herself from rolling her eyes. Somehow, the same lines Rae had used were offensive here in the real world. Or maybe it was the delivery. Or, more likely, the deliverer.

"Fortunately, I'm not the best one to ask about that." She smiled mysteriously, hoping Gretchen would let it go at that.

"Yeah, you should have seen Cori in Vegas." Julie had to go there. "First day we're poolside and she has a local dealer falling all over her."

Lisa pushed her plate away. "I love Vegas. Even if you don't gamble, there's so much to do."

"What was your favorite part, Cori?" Gretchen asked.

This question gave her pause. The real answer—her favorite part was the time she spent with Rae—was not the answer others were looking for. She shrugged. "I enjoyed all of it."

"Cori tried out for a band." Julie tipped her glass toward Cori. "Tell 'em about it, Cor."

"I think you have a better memory of it than I do. I'd had way too many of those blue drinks by the pool."

"You're a singer?" Gretchen asked.

Cori cursed herself for not being open to this woman. So far she'd been a perfect date. She brought flowers, opened the door, asked polite, probing questions. She'd made more than one suggestive overture, but they were adults. Women over thirty were known to have sex occasionally. Sometimes, if they were lucky, they made it with each other. She couldn't fault Gretchen for making her wishes known. Yet, despite all the apparent pluses, she could not find any enthusiasm for Gretchen's company.

"I sing sometimes," she replied damply, hoping the topic would lose its charm for her companions.

"You never did tell me what they said about the audition," Julie said. "They were supposed to get back to you."

The waiter dropped off the check, thankfully creating a diversion. Cori didn't know what she was going to do with Kel's offer, so why dwell on it?

"What kind of music do you sing?" Lisa asked.

"Oh, you should have heard this one song." Julie fished her wallet out of her pocket. "What was it? The Nina Simone song?"

"'Since I Fell for You.'"

"I love that song." Gretchen slipped her card into the holder with the bill. "You should sing it for us."

Did Gretchen even know who Nina Simone was? Chalk up another reason to like her if she did. Julie was right. Gretchen might very well be perfect for her.

Lisa squealed and clapped. "Yes. You have to. They have karaoke until nine. I bet you could get in."

Cori gulped down the last of her rum—her fourth—filling time until the waiter returned with Gretchen and Julie's cards and receipts.

Gretchen rose and offered her hand. Cori let herself be led into the lounge, pushing back thoughts of the last time she sang this song, with Rae huddled in the corner, trying not to be noticed. Cori had been surprised when Rae commented on it; her memory of the audition was hazy. But when she thought back now, she could picture the glow of a cigarette in the dim light. A lean figure in the shadows. Rae, watching her.

Gretchen finished talking to the DJ and joined Cori at the table. "I can't believe they actually have it. You're up next." After a brief hesitation, she took Cori's hand.

Cori smiled, letting her fingers lie limp in Gretchen's. "Great."

Far too soon, the woman on stage finished dismantling "She Thinks My Tractor's Sexy" and Cori was propelled to the front amidst good-natured hoots and whistles from her table mates. She stood, microphone in hand, willing the music not to start. Of course, it did and she surrendered to it. She couldn't look at Gretchen as she sang. It seemed calloused and harsh to look at one woman while singing about another.

She poured herself, her confusion, her desire, her burned out heart, into the words. When she finished, the room was silent. No clinking glasses. No rowdy bar laughter. Nothing. Every face stared up at her, mouths slightly open in beer-enhanced awe. Gretchen broke into the moment, her loud whistle piercing the tension.

"Damn, you can sing," she enthused as she walked Cori back to the table and held out her chair.

Cori didn't sit. "I need to go." She gathered up her belongings and made apologies. "I'm sorry. I just remembered I have an early morning. You all stay. I'll catch a cab."

She didn't give them a choice as she rushed through her departure. She needed to get away, be alone with her thoughts of Rae. She didn't want anyone else, so why even try?

Gretchen chased her to the door. "Cori, wait." She put her hand on her arm. "I enjoyed tonight and I'd like to do it again. Call me, okay?" She produced a business card and scribbled a number on it. "That's my cell."

The look on Gretchen's face said she wanted more than a hasty kiss on the cheek, but it was all Cori could manage. The parking lot was full of dykes out for a good time. Cori looked up at the night sky. The neon lights of Vegas seemed as far away as the stars above her, out of reach no matter how high she jumped.

Rae's love, Cori knew, would always be like that, just outside her grasp. Cori would drive her away, not draw her closer. Women like Rae couldn't handle a lover who was desperate and clinging, and Cori could see herself hanging on that way. Not trusting that she was loved.

Gretchen was here. Now. And more than willing to help her forget, if only for the night. Rae wouldn't even hesitate. She'd have Gretchen up against her car in the parking lot, making her scream for all of greater Seattle to hear. Wasn't that what she did the night before? With Sharon and Dar? She'd tried to fuck Cori out of her system. And still she'd called Cori, strung tight and in need of release.

Cori wasn't going to wait while Rae figured out what she wanted. Her heart couldn't take it. She turned toward the door of the lounge to see Gretchen waiting there, watching. She started walking.

Gretchen met her halfway, her lips open to the hard invasion of Cori's tongue.

"Take me home," Cori said, feeling cheap. "Your place."

Cori flipped Gretchen and ran one finger down her spine. The lack of any real passion made her increasingly aggressive and Gretchen proportionately more responsive.

"God," Gretchen panted, the blanket gripped tight in her fingers, her toes curled tight. "You're so fucking hot."

Cori nipped the taut skin of Gretchen's lower back, then slid her tongue along the crease between Gretchen's cheeks. Gretchen shivered. From behind, with the lights down and her eyes closed, Cori could almost imagine Gretchen was Rae.

Almost.

She gripped Gretchen's hips, urging her up on all fours, and ground her pelvis into Gretchen's ass. *This isn't Rae* played through her mind on constant refrain, muting the experience and keeping her passion from flaring hot. She bent at the waist, curling over Gretchen, and dragged her nipples across the firm back beneath her.

Gretchen arched against her and Cori held her tight. Close to her ear, she asked, "Do you have a cock?"

There was no way she was going to come tonight. Not with Gretchen. Not like this. But there was no reason Gretchen shouldn't enjoy herself.

Gretchen nodded—urgent, fevered.

"Do you want me to use it?" Cori circled her hips slowly against Gretchen, pressing hard.

"God, yes." Gretchen started to pull away, moving toward the edge of the bed.

"No." Cori held her firm. "Stay here. I'll get it."

Gretchen dropped her head to the mattress, her ass high, legs spread, her pink center dripping. Cori retrieved the toy from the drawer Gretchen pointed to and slipped into the leather harness. It'd been a long time since she'd used one and she planned to fuck Gretchen hard enough to chase Rae's image away. She grabbed a small bottle of lube and climbed back on the bed, the purple silicone bobbing between her legs.

She squirted lube on her fingers and worked her hand up and down the cock. She liked the way it felt. If she had a real one, she'd never get anything done. She'd simply stay home and stroke it all day long.

Gretchen edged backward, begging. Cori placed the purple tip at her opening, but didn't push in.

Gretchen moaned. "Please."

"You want this." Cori wriggled slightly, one hand on Gretchen's back, the other around the dildo, holding it just outside.

Gretchen pushed against Cori. "Yes."

Cori moved her hands to their earlier position on Gretchen's hips and eased forward. Slow and steady, feeling her way, she pushed into Gretchen, stretching her. Gretchen looked back over her shoulder. Her face danced the line between pain and ecstasy.

Cori stopped. "Can you take it all?"

"Yes. Just…easy," Gretchen choked out between gritted teeth. "More."

Cori gripped Gretchen's ass and massaged the wet parting with her thumbs, relaxing it, coaxing her open. Then she pushed until she was all in with Gretchen's pussy stretched around her. The base of the cock pressed against Cori's clit. She kept her front tight against Gretchen's trembling backside, then eased out until just the head remained inside.

"Are you ready to be fucked?"

Gretchen's voice shook. "Yes."

Cori stroked in deep, filling her completely, then pulling back. She rode her harder with each plunge until sweat dripped from her and pooled in the dip of Gretchen's spine.

"Oh, God, please. Fuck me," Gretchen panted.

Cori pushed harder, but still Rae's face swam in front of her.

"Yes."

Faster. She felt Rae's breath on her thighs.

"Just like that."

Deeper. And Rae was inside of her, fucking her, coaxing her.

Gretchen slammed back into her, pressing tight as she quaked through her orgasm. Cori held her and moaned out a faked climax. Rae's teasing laughter echoed in her head. *Come back to Vegas, Cori. I'll make you scream loud enough to wake up the neighborhood. You'll never have to fake it again.*

"God." Gretchen collapsed and the cock slid out of her with a pop.

Cori headed toward the bathroom, stepping out of the harness as she went.

"You can leave that on the sink," Gretchen called. "I'll take care of it later."

Cori washed the lube from her hands and did as she was told. The purple dildo looked vulgar against the sterile white tile. With a heavy sigh she returned to the bedroom and collected her clothes.

"Hey, you don't have to rush off." Gretchen looked hurt.

"Yeah. I do." Cori stepped into her panties and slipped her dress over her head. Guilt settled around her with the fabric. She'd used Gretchen. The quicker she got home and washed the smell of sex from her skin, the better.

"Hey, sit down." Gretchen urged her onto the edge of the bed. "Relax a moment."

She reached out for Cori's hand, almost as though expecting a rebuff. Cori allowed the tentative clasp, curling her fingers lightly around Gretchen's. Holding hands felt surprisingly chaste given their recent activities.

"Want to tell me about it?" Gretchen asked.

Cori didn't. She shook her head.

"Cori, you're a great fuck. No doubt about it." Regret laced Gretchen's words, as though she already knew this would be their first and last encounter. "But it's not worth it if it makes you feel like this afterward."

"How do you know what I feel?" Cori knew she sounded like a petulant child. All that was missing was arms tightly folded and the stomp of her foot. She held herself stiffly, resisting the urge.

"Well, I think it's pretty safe to say that tonight isn't about love for either of us."

Cori laughed bitterly. Gretchen was wrong. Cori was pretty sure that's exactly what it was about. "I used you."

"And I used you." Gretchen released her hand. "What's the problem?"

Cori tried again. "I fucked you."

Gretchen laughed. "Yes, you did. And I thank you for that."

"But I was thinking about someone else."

"Ah." Gretchen gave a small smile. "The crux of the matter."

Cori didn't know what else to say. For all the nice bonding and sharing, she still wanted a shower. And Rae.

"I had a woman like that once. Made me forget everything but her."

"What happened?"

"We lived together for ten years." Gretchen looked at the wall. "She died last year. Cancer."

"Oh, Christ." What can of worms had she opened? "I'm sorry."

"Tonight was my first date since..."

"And you got *me*." Cori sagged. All the air fizzed from her self-absorbed anger. She sat down on the edge of the bed. "I'm sorry, Gretchen."

"It's okay. Truth be told, I wasn't thinking about you either."

Cori laughed. "Well, aren't we a pair?"

"There's not a moment with her that I don't wish I could get back," Gretchen said forlornly. "Even the screaming fights. The annoying habits. All of it. I'd trade everything for just one more day. In her arms, life was worth living."

They sat together in silence. Cori wanted to say something comforting to help Gretchen not feel her loss so vividly. But words like that didn't exist, she was sure. "She sounds very special."

"She was." Gretchen took her hand again. "If you have

even the slightest chance at love like that, you have to grab it and not let go. It's worth it. Every miserable, unbearable, blissful moment is worth it."

Cori's breath seemed trapped in her chest. Her throat refused to open. Did she have a chance for that kind of love? An all-consuming, life-spanning love...with Rae? Only a fool wouldn't find out.

She was going back. She had found Rae and wouldn't let her slip away.

CHAPTER FOURTEEN

The Warhol-style painting of three lucky sevens seemed oddly out of sync with the rest of the conservative furnishings in the room. Rae breathed in the scent of leather and wood polish as she shook Ed Rashner's hand. His grip was firm, reminiscent of his good ol' boy Texas upbringing.

"It's a pleasure to meet you, sir." Rae held herself back, terrified that her wide-eyed excitement would show through. "I can't believe I'm here."

She'd spent the morning in front of the mirror, wrestling her facial features under control. As soon as she'd managed a weak vestige of calm, the thrill of being summoned to the vice president's office would spring to the surface again.

"The pleasure's mine, Rae." He gestured toward a high back leather chair. "Have a seat."

Ed Rashner wore his smile like a hard-won commodity. Rae guessed that it had once been charming, back when he was a ranch hand in the Lone Star State. Now he had a salesman's polish, the look of a man who made his living off the poor impulse control of others. How many mornings had he stood in front of his own mirror perfecting that look?

"Did Greg tell you why I requested this meeting?" He leaned against the corner of his great mahogany desk, one hand resting on a thick manila folder.

"No, sir. He just said you wished to speak with me." Rae felt her bangs slipping into her eyes and tucked them behind her ear.

Mr. Rashner picked up the file and flipped it open. "You've worked for us for quite some time now. Your mother, too."

Rae nodded, unsure where this was going.

"During that time, you've attended classes, working toward a BA in business management. Is that correct?"

"Right."

"And you've been vocal about your interest in one day occupying my office." He closed the file. "What do you say, should we start that journey today?"

Rae's mouth fell open and she snapped it shut, her teeth jarring together. "I don't understand, sir."

"We have an opening, starting in a few weeks, for a pit boss on days. It's the first step on the ladder." Mr. Rashner looked pleased, sure of himself.

Rae let her smile loose. This was it, the offer she'd been working for. It would mean a change in her class schedule, but that was a technicality, certainly not an obstacle. She couldn't wait to tell her mom, to tell Cori.

Cori. Who lived in Seattle.

Her confidence faltered.

She'd always wanted the glittering bells and whistles of the Las Vegas Strip. As a child she huddled beneath her mom's table, church mouse quiet, as the cards were doled out, one after another. The hypnotic sound of the shuffler lulled her to sleep and she'd dreamed of smoke-filled rooms, spinning numbers, and glittering sequins until her mom gathered her up and carried her home to finish the night.

Then her grandmother—bitter over the wasted life of her only son, Rae's absentee father—had asked, "Rae, what will you be when you grow up?" The condemning judgment dared her to be useful, to not disappoint.

"I'm going to work with mommy, at the casino." Rae had been sure that was a good answer. Mommy liked her job. She laughed and played games all night long.

Her grandmother, old even then, had tapped her cane against the floor. "No. If you work in a casino, you run the casino. Nothing else will do."

Rae had nodded, soaking up the rare smile on her grandmother's face.

"Well, Rae?" Mr. Rashner's voice brought Rae out of her memories. "What do you say?"

A month ago, Rae would have jumped on the offer. "I'm not sure, sir."

"What?"

Rae backpedaled, her sense of self-preservation kicking in one sentence too late. "I'm flattered. And of course I'm interested. I would just like to talk over the offer with a couple of people. This is not a small decision and I want to make the right one."

The move to day shift would have a financial impact due to loss of tips. The increase in pay had to be significant enough to offset that and make the increase in responsibility worthwhile. This mix of pros and cons made the day shift the most difficult to fill. When someone like Rae, who was looking to climb high, was ready for promotion, it was a blessing for both the casino and the employee. Still, she could hide behind the money as a reason for delaying her decision. She needed to talk to her mom. And, if she could manage it, she needed to talk to Cori.

Mr. Rashner's smile returned in full, dazzling Rae with a row of perfect white caps. "Of course. I understand the financial considerations. Take a couple of days. But this matter needs to be resolved by Wednesday."

"Fine." Rae stood, shook his outstretched hand, and retreated to the elevator.

Wednesday gave her a full day longer than she needed. A quick stop at her mom's house, followed by a night of clutching the phone, trying to work up the nerve to dial Cori's number. Before she could decide anything, she had to know where the two of them were going.

❖

Norma squealed and threw her arms around Rae. "The old bastard finally offered you a promotion, huh?"

Rae detangled herself and took a sip of her tea. "Yep, looks like."

Norma narrowed her eyes. "Why aren't you more excited?"

Rae sidestepped the question by asking one of her own. "Why do you love Vegas?"

"Oh, honey, I don't. Sometimes I hate this damn city."

"You don't like Vegas? I thought…" Rae was stunned. "Then why did you stay?"

"Because I love you and the work was here." Norma pulled out a chair at the kitchen table, her eyes drifting as she thought back. "Finding work as a single mom is not easy to do. It was even harder back then. And your grandmother, old dragon that she was, promised to help."

"You realize this changes my entire outlook. I grew up loving Vegas because of you. All my memories are tied up with casinos and lights."

Norma rested her elbows on the flat, wooden tabletop. "It

hasn't been a bad life, Rae. Those memories, and the love, that's all real."

Rae nodded, not convinced.

"So." Norma shifted back to talk of the promotion. "When do you start the new job?"

"I'm not sure. I told him I have to think about it."

"Rae, what's going on in that head of yours?" Norma mussed Rae's hair, a move only a mother could get away with.

"Cori."

"Nice girl, I like her. You should bring her by again."

"She's gone."

"Gone?"

"Back to Seattle, where she lives."

Rae stared out the sliding glass door. Sunlight glinted off the water in Norma's rarely used pool. Did Cori like to swim?

"Is that what this is about?"

"She's all I think about."

Norma gave an impatient huff. "So, go and get her."

Such simple words. *Go and get her.* If only life could be pared down to a four-word sentence. "It's not that easy, Mom."

"Do you love her?"

There it was, the question of the ages. Was she in love with Cori? If this wasn't love, the real thing would kill her completely. "I think so."

"Then it *is* that easy." Norma brushed her hands together like she was dusting them off. "What else is there but love?"

"She wants more than I can give." Was that true? She knew exactly what to give Cori in the bedroom, but did she know what Cori wanted from life? She'd never asked.

"And what is that?" Norma put her on the spot, which wasn't unusual.

"I think she wants happily ever after."

"And what do you want?"

Rae paused. The answer was so simple before Cori. She'd wanted a fast life, the big office, and easy women. Now, all she could think about was cuddling with Cori beneath the covers. "I don't know," she whispered.

"What's wrong with having a relationship?"

"Nothing, I'm just not sure I'm relationship material."

"How will you ever know if you don't try?"

Was that what her father did? Tried and found out too late, after a wife and child were part of the equation? Rae refused to be like him. "I won't make a promise I can't keep."

Norma circled the table and drew Rae into a hug. "Sweetie, you don't have to. Just let the relationship happen. Let yourself be happy."

"Isn't that what happened to you and Dad? He left to be happy?"

Rae had never questioned Norma about her relationship with her dad before. In fact, they rarely discussed him beyond bullet point updates. *He's in California. He's doing well. He said to tell you hi.* Nothing more.

Rae didn't tell her mom about the time he'd called her for bail money. Or that his current girlfriend was younger than Rae. Or that he showed up at her apartment every few years, drunk and begging forgiveness for being such a bad father. He never remembered her birthday. He'd smashed her piggy bank with a hammer when she was eight, taking every last nickel. She hadn't seen him again after that visit until she turned eleven. She didn't mention to her mom that the only time he called her at Christmas was when he needed something. Or that he was banned from the casino for tying to snatch a stack of chips from Rae's table, demanding that she owed him for all the sacrifices he'd made for her. She'd almost lost her job over that incident. Thankfully she'd been able to convince loss prevention that even though he was her father, she wasn't in collusion with him. She still puzzled over the sacrifices he claimed to have made on her behalf.

No, those things she kept locked away for herself. She'd bring out the memories and nibble on them anytime she was feeling sorry that she didn't see more of him. The sharp edges kept her from calling him.

Norma's eyes hardened. "You are *not* your father."

"How do you know?"

"I married the man. I know who he is."

No arguing with that. Rae sipped her drink cautiously. "Tell me honestly. Am I like him?"

"Is that what you fear?" Norma asked astutely.

"Maybe."

"You have parts of him…the good parts. The sun comes out when you're around. You get that from him. But he has too much charisma for a man with weak character. He was selfish and shortsighted. You're neither of those things. You have self-discipline. He doesn't."

Rae had listened to her mom cry through the bedroom door more than once when she was little. Those tears always coincided with her dad's arrival and subsequent departure. Rae refused to do that to another person, especially Cori. She couldn't bear to let down the people who loved her, so she hesitated to make a commitment. What if she promised forever and woke up after a year, or two, stifled and suffocating, unable to resist the need to run? Just like her father.

"You are not him," her mom repeated.

"How do you know that for sure?"

"Because I know you, Rae. I know your heart." She took Rae's hand in hers and pressed it to Rae's chest. "You're good deep down. You take care of the people you love, and there's room in your heart for one more. Don't let fear of your father keep you from grabbing what you want with both hands."

"What if she doesn't want to live in Vegas?"

"Then you move to Seattle. Small things like where you live are only details in the face of love." Norma kissed Rae's head. "Love, *real* love, can't be denied. If you try, it'll eat you up inside."

Rae was struck by her mother's words. The gnawing hole in her gut grew larger with each passing day. Promotion be damned. She needed to be with Cori, one way or another.

Caller ID revealed that Kel had called twice while Cori was at work but didn't leave a voice mail. Cori tapped the readout. Should she call back or wait until Kel called again? Before she could decide, the phone rang in her hand.

"Cori, glad I caught you." Kel's tone bordered between sarcastic amusement and genuine interest. The combination left Cori unsure of what to say next.

"What's the word? You gonna come play with us or what?"

All the reasons for hesitating fell away. Kel was offering exactly what she needed, an escape from her workaday life in Seattle, an opportunity to chase her American Dream. Even if she forgot about Rae completely, which had proven impossible so far, her future happiness hinged on the answer to one simple question. Did Cori want to move to Las Vegas and join Kel's band? Crazy and fanciful? Maybe. But there was only one answer she could give.

"Yes." Cori dropped into the nearest chair, the impact of one word crumbling her at the knees.

"Yes?" Kel sounded unsure.

"Yes. Absolutely."

"When can you be here?"

"Give me a week."

Cori half-listened to the rest of the conversation, scribbling down information she might need later. God help her, she was moving to Vegas.

Rae folded and unfolded the mangled piece of casino stationery that had Cori's home and cell phone numbers written on it. Twice she'd made it as high as the sixth number. She'd hung up both times before punching in the seventh. She took a deep breath and tried again. The phone rang four times then went to voice mail. Odd. Eight o'clock on a Monday night. Cori should be home from work.

Rae toyed with the idea of simply putting her thoughts down in an e-mail. No. She'd come this far, she couldn't punk out now. Maybe she could reach her on her cell phone.

Cori answered on the third ring, her greeting reserved. "Hello, Rae."

"Cori? Is everything okay?"

"Long day." Cori paused. "Did you go to another party?"

Was that why Cori didn't answer her home phone? Jealousy?

"What? No." This conversation would be much easier in person, if she were able to look in Cori's eyes, hold her in her arms. "I need to talk to you about work."

"Work?" Cori snorted. "Since when do we talk about work?"

Ouch. Cori wasn't going to make this easy.

"Let me start over." Rae pushed her fingers through her hair. "I can't stop thinking about you. No matter what I'm doing, you're there."

Cori didn't respond. The soft sound of her breathing assured Rae she was still on the line.

"My boss has offered me a promotion, but I put him off. I can't stay here without you. If you're in Seattle, then that's where I want to be."

Rae's head pounded with the confession as she waited for Cori to say something, anything. Still she remained silent.

"I'm sure I could find work there. Not in a casino, obviously. But there are hotels and such. I don't know, there has to be something I can do." She was babbling. She could feel it, but she couldn't leave the dead air between them. She charged forward, her good judgment screeching at her to shut up, for the love of God. "Cori, it's up to you. If you want me there, I'm yours."

She stopped, abruptly out of words. She'd said everything that mattered. Still no response from Cori. "Cori? Did you hear what I said?"

"Yes," Cori said softly.

"I'll have to give notice, of course. And I probably shouldn't move until I actually have a job, but I'll start—"

"Rae, stop." Cori interrupted. "Take the promotion. There's no reason for you to move to Seattle."

"What?" Rae's heart fell out of her chest and landed with a dull thunk on the carpet at her feet. Surely she was hearing things. No way would Cori respond with such indifference. "But..." Rae stopped. She'd offered her love, her life, to Cori and she'd said no. No amount of discussion would change that. "Okay. I'm sorry, Cori, I won't call you again."

Rae closed her cell phone against Cori's hasty protests.

There was nothing Cori could say to erase the hurt that came with her rejection.

Her phone rang a few seconds later and she didn't pick up. After the fifth time, she turned it off and stuffed it under the sofa cushion. Then she lay down and cried, the heartache flowing from her and taking root in the air, the furniture, the very building around her.

Tomorrow she would dry her eyes, drive to work, and accept the promotion. Tonight she deserved her tears.

CHAPTER FIFTEEN

A wave of nausea swept over Rae and the rising pressure behind her eyes promised her head would explode before much longer. She gripped the fold-up arms attached to her seat as the plane banked left and descended toward the runway. No matter how many times she flew, she never quite got used to the change in pressure during takeoff and landing.

Norma covered Rae's hand with her own and gave it a gentle pat. "Almost there, sweetie."

Rae swallowed. "Yep."

"Tell me again why you won't take Dramamine."

The laughter in Norma's eyes belied the concern in her voice. Rae stared down the aisle and didn't answer. Norma knew the why. Dramamine knocked Rae out. Not a little drowsy but head back, mouth open, drool down her chin, snoring to the rafters knocked out. So the question was not asked out of concern. She just couldn't pass on an opportunity to torment her.

After far too long, the plane touched down and the pressure in Rae's head eased. She rubbed her eyes. "Kills me every time."

"Factoring out the takeoff and landing, you had a good time. Right, honey?"

After Cori's rejection, Norma had somehow convinced Greg to authorize an impromptu vacation for Rae, claiming that it would be much more difficult for her to use her vacation time once she stepped into her new position. They'd spent the last week lounging on the beach in Mazatlan. No neon, no blackjack, nothing to remind Rae of Las Vegas. But it didn't keep her from thinking of Cori.

"Yeah, I had a good time."

Rae couldn't tell her mom that all she'd gained from the trip was a great tan. The ache in her heart hadn't eased. In fact, the entire time she was there, she'd compared every woman she saw to Cori. None of them stacked up. For the first time in her life, Rae had actually said no to a beautiful woman. More than once.

She retrieved their carry-ons from the overhead compartment and followed Norma to the exit. They weaved through the ceaseless bustle of the Las Vegas airport and caught the tram to baggage claim.

"It's going to be okay, honey," Norma said. "Broken hearts don't last forever."

Several heads turned her direction as her mom patted her hand. The strangers' eyes were full of sympathy.

"Can we save this conversation for later?" It was Rae's standard answer whenever Norma broached the subject.

"You have to talk about it eventually."

The tram glided to a stop and Rae stepped out without answering.

Norma didn't give up. "Honey, please. I'm worried about you."

Rae kept walking, her attention focused straight ahead.

"And I appreciate that, Mom. Really I do. But I'd rather not talk about it in front of strangers."

Norma looked around, seeming to take in her surroundings for the first time. "Oh."

They stopped in front of the luggage carousel. The red light blinked, announcing the impending arrival of their bags, and the conveyor started moving.

"I'm sorry." Norma heaved a sigh. "I don't mean to embarrass you."

"It's okay."

"I'm just worried about you."

"I'm *okay*."

Rae's bag came into view.

"Rae…"

"Mom. I'm hot. I'm tired. And my head is pounding. Please, just let me go home."

Rae picked up her bag, kissed her mom on the cheek, and headed toward the door. Norma stared after her as she climbed aboard the shuttle to long-term parking, but she didn't return Rae's wave good-bye.

Her mother would forgive her, she hoped, for leaving her to get her own bag. Rae rested her head against the seat in front of her and squeezed the back of her neck, willing the thumping in her head to subside. She just needed to get back to her life. She would be busy with school and work, too busy to keep dwelling on what would never be.

The usually comforting silence in her apartment taunted Rae, driving home the message that she was unquestionably and unchangingly alone. She pushed play on her CD player without checking to see which artist was coming up. She was more interested in filling the sound vacuum than listening to music. Then she adjusted the thermostat to seventy-four, unpacked, poured herself a drink, and checked her e-mail, deleting six messages from Cori without reading them. Being told no over the phone was enough. Rae didn't need a Dear John letter on top of it.

The light on her answering machine blinked. Twenty-two messages. She didn't even want to listen to them, but pushed the play button just in case something important had happened in the week she was gone.

"Rae, it's Cori—"

Delete.

"Rae, please, I need—"

Delete.

"Rae, you can't—"

Delete.

Twenty-one of twenty-two messages were from Cori, the level of desperation in her voice increasing with each one. The only other person who'd called was Kel. Rae listened to that one.

"Dude, come by the club and check in. We're back at work and the place doesn't rock the same without you"

Rae collapsed onto her couch, legs up, head against the arm, and held a throw pillow over her eyes. She refused to cry just because Cori had called. Crying sucked. Cori sucked. Las Vegas sucked. Love sucked. Life sucked.

With a frustrated growl, she threw the pillow across the room. It hit the window and fell to the floor with an impotent *poof*.

"Fuck this." Rae moved her self-indulgent pity party to the bathroom and splashed water on her face. Her eyes were red and puffy, and her hair stood on end. Even the long front part refused to behave.

She jammed a ball cap on her head, grabbed her keys, and headed toward the club. It wasn't where she wanted to be, but what was new? The only place she wanted to be—in Cori's arms—was the one place she couldn't be. There was no point in moping at home when she could be out with friends.

She tapped a Camel out of her pack and lit it as she stepped into the dim light of the club. The swinging door whooshed shut behind her, blocking out the hail of protests from the people waiting in line to get in. Let 'em scream. She was here long before they arrived and she'd be here long after they went back to their lives. The bouncer on the door knew it. They had that in common.

She stopped two steps in, slack-jawed, cigarette clinging to her lip, and stared at the stage in disbelief.

Cori.

A long black dress hugged her body, the neck cut so low that just a little nudge from Rae's tongue and those beautiful nipples would be hers, hard and ready. The fabric shimmered as she danced. A slit went from the hem to high on her hip, inviting long looks at the leg provocatively displayed. Her eyes were closed and she cupped the mic kissing-close to her lips. She swayed to the band's cover version of Melissa Ferrick's "Drive" with the same intimate, pulsing rhythm she used when making love.

Rae stumbled back, bumping into faceless people as she groped for the wall behind her. Cori's voice washed over her and she slumped against the solid surface, helpless and unable to move, to run. To Cori. Or away from her.

Cori wasn't in Seattle. She was here. Or was she? Rae took a shaky drag of her cigarette and rubbed her eyes with the heels of her hands. No amount of tired, bloodshot, smoke-filled vision would make her hallucinate Cori, would it?

Coming here was a bad idea. Rae turned toward the door as the song came to an end. Cori was here for the band, not for her. She had moved to Las Vegas for music, not for Rae. Wanting Cori and not being able have her while she was in Seattle had killed Rae. But wanting her and not being able to have her while she was in Vegas? Rae couldn't think, couldn't breathe.

Cori was flirting with the crowd, winking at a leggy brunette close to the stage. She paused and cast a long look deep into the room. Rae forced her legs to move as Cori's gaze met hers. Cori's smile faded and she raised her hand in a jerky flutter. Dazed and desperate to wake up from this nightmare, Rae shook her head and ran for the door.

Kel counted the next song in and Cori fumbled for the lyrics. She sang reflexively. The words tasted like cardboard and lay dead on her tongue. She closed her eyes against the churning emotion building low in her belly.

She'd left Rae countless messages, enough that she was sure she'd broken some sort of anti-stalking laws, but she still couldn't stop calling. Rae never called back, not even to say so much as a *fuck you*. And it was too late by then to change her mind about moving. The wheels were in motion and whether Rae wanted her or not, she'd said yes to Kel. And the truth was, she wanted to make the move. It was time, and there was no backing out of that commitment. She owed herself the possibility of a life that meant more, even without the woman she wanted to share it with.

Yet the look on Rae's face just moments ago, when Cori

looked up from flirting with her audience. Oh, God, Rae saw her wink at that brunette. She'd not been prepared to see Cori, that was obvious from the complete stunned shock on her face. But how could she not know? Yes, she'd asked Kel not to say anything, to let her surprise Rae with the news. But she'd left so many messages and shared all the details, Rae had to know.

Cori finished the set in a daze and walked off stage while the crowd was still clapping. She had to call Rae. Now.

Four rings. Voice mail. She dialed again. "Rae...I... Fuck."

She ended the call. She couldn't say what she needed to say to a machine.

The noise of the others filtered down the steps toward the dressing room. Cori stripped in a hurry and pulled on her street clothes. Normally she'd take the time to remove her makeup before heading out. Tonight she couldn't afford even the few minutes the post-performance ritual would take. She hiked her bag over her shoulder and retraced her steps back up the stairs, passing Kel and the others as she went.

"What's the rush, Cori?"

Someone laughed. "Didn't you see her? The brunette with the legs, right?"

"Stay awhile," Kel said. "We're going to party. You can invite her back."

Cori forced a smile, but never slowed on her journey toward Rae. "Sorry, guys. Not tonight. I have some things to take care of."

"You sure? She's hot for you."

"I'm sure."

Nobody, no matter how long her legs or how sexy her curves, would convince Cori to stay. She needed to get to Rae. Thankfully she had her address.

Chapter Sixteen

Rae sat stunned on her sofa, a mental Cori checklist playing on constant loop in her head.

Cori was in Las Vegas.

Cori didn't want her.

Cori was flirting with that woman. Not her.

She stared at the bottle of tequila on the low table in front of her. She'd screwed the lid off and back on at least six times. She opened it again. All the sun and sand in Mexico couldn't make her forget Cori and didn't ease the pain. Would a drink that smelled like rancid piss really help? No. She returned the cap to the bottle.

The pain, sharp and fresh, was hers. It might have been all she could have of Cori, but she owned it and she wasn't ready to give it up.

The doorbell rang. Again. And again. Followed by a frantic knocking

"Rae. Open the door. Please, let me in," Cori pleaded.

Rae didn't move. "Why?" She cleared her throat and said it again, louder. "Why? Why should I let you in?"

She'd tried that already. It hurt too much to try again so soon.

"Please, we need to talk." More thuds sounded against the

door. "I just have to see you. Please…let me in. Let me touch you."

Rae's fingers ached in time with the dull throbbing in her head. Her whole body hurt. Her skin hummed with need, with the knowledge that Cori was here and asking for her. Finally, against the screaming caution in her mind, she crossed to the door and threw it open.

Cori stood there, bag at her feet, stage makeup streaked down her face, wearing jeans and a T-shirt instead of the killer "sex me up" dress from earlier. Rae held herself rigid against her warring emotions. Part of her wanted to pull Cori close to her, part of her wanted to slam the door, and part of her wanted to charge past Cori, back to the club to put the smackdown on the woman Cori had been flirting with. *Mine, mine, mine.* Jealousy was an ugly, ugly emotion.

She stepped back and motioned for Cori to come in. Cori took half a step toward her but Rae held up her hand.

"No." No touching. She'd never survive it. "You said you wanted to talk."

They moved to the couch, sitting carefully apart from one another. Rae waited.

Cori looked around. "I've never been here before."

"Is that why you came here, Cori?" Rae started to stand. "Just curiosity?"

"No!" Cori grabbed Rae's hand, pulling her back down. "No, please. Just wait."

Rae looked at their entwined grip and extricated herself, one finger at a time.

"Why are you doing this?" Cori folded her hands in her lap. "You said you wanted me." Her voice got smaller as she spoke. "You said you couldn't stop thinking of me. Of being with me. And now…this."

Rae pressed her fingers to her closed eyelids. Being this

close to Cori and not touching her was just too hard. Still, she held herself back. "You said no."

"I said no?" Cori sounded confused.

"You said no, don't move to Seattle, don't come to me. Take the job, there's nothing here for you." Rae hated the words. Hated being forced to say them aloud.

"You hung up before—"

"What else was there to say? You didn't want me. Why hang around after that?"

Cori placed one hand on either side of Rae's head and turned her face toward her. "I never said that, Rae." Her voice was gentle.

"Yes." Rae searched her memory, certain of Cori's message. "You did."

"No. I wouldn't say that, because I do want you. Why would I say I don't when I do?"

Because you're an evil fucking sadist and you're trying to kill me. Rae knew that wasn't true. Cori was kind and sweet. Loving. Definitely not sadistic.

"Didn't you get my messages?" Cori asked.

"No."

"Oh, Rae, no wonder you're so mad at me."

Cori leaned in for a kiss, sad laughter in her eyes. Rae was almost there, so close to letting Cori kiss her concerns away. But just like the tequila, that kiss couldn't wipe the slate clean. Maybe Cori's touch would dull the pain, possibly enough for Rae to forget that she would be kicked in the teeth the next morning when Cori walked away.

She turned her head at the last moment. "No. You don't get to kiss me like nothing's wrong."

"Rae, I'm here. Right here. In Vegas. Why would I want you to move to Seattle? Of course I told you not to. By then I knew I was coming. Don't you see?"

Light flooded Rae. When she was babbling about moving to Seattle, Cori was already planning to move to Las Vegas? How could she not have figured that out? She cast her mind back, recalling the way she'd slammed the phone down on Cori's protests. Then left town for a week to lick her wounds.

"Your voice mail messages…" The ones she had deleted without listening to.

"You were gone when I got here," Cori said, plainly bewildered. "Your mom was gone. Nobody knew where you were. I was frantic."

"You looked frantic tonight, flirting with that woman." Oh, God, pouting and jealous were not attractive.

Cori threw up her hands. "I'm an entertainer. That was an *act*."

Act or not, Rae didn't like it. Still, she didn't want Cori to know exactly how irrational it made her. Was this how Cori felt when she saw Rae with other women? A sledgehammer hit Rae in the chest. She'd thought Cori was being petty when she made that crack about her going to another party. Now she understood.

"I'm sorry I slept with those other women."

Cori cringed. "We don't need to talk about that."

"No, really. I'm sorry. I hate that it hurt you."

"Don't apologize, Rae. It's who you are. That's just something I have to accept."

Really? Was that who Rae really was, deep down? Rae shook her head, realization climbing to the surface. "I don't think so. I think that's who I let myself be because it was easier."

Cori didn't look convinced.

"My mom took me to Mexico," Rae said. "A week surrounded by beautiful Latinas and they all reminded me of you. I didn't have sex once."

Cori opened her mouth and closed it, shook her head, then laughed. "I'm going to kiss you now and you don't get to stop me."

Rae's breath caught in her throat as Cori cupped her cheek, her thumb smoothing over Rae's lips. She stared at Cori's mouth and waited, a shiver tripping over her skin. Slowly, gently, Cori kissed her. No hurry, no urgent push. Just the sweet, flowing press of her lips as Rae lost herself in the knowledge that she was in love. She loved Cori. She couldn't help it.

Cori leaned back and smiled, her eyes tender and sparkling.

"I'm scared." Rae put it all out there. "I think I…love you. What if this doesn't work?"

"It will." Cori sounded certain.

"Really?"

"It may not, but we have to try. Because I think I love you, too."

"My father ran away after promising forever. What if I do the same thing?" It hurt to say that to Cori, but she deserved to know what she could be in for.

"My father stayed and tortured my family. Is that better?"

Rae tucked her arm around Cori, snuggling closer. "I don't know."

They sat silently for several beats, letting the future gather before them.

"What if you sleep with someone else?" Cori asked.

"I won't." Rae, for all her philandering, was confident.

"But what if I want you to?" Cori laughed uncomfortably. Her skin was too dark to see a blush, but Rae swore she could hear it in her voice.

"Are you blushing?"

Cori shook her head hard. "No. Absolutely not."

Rae squeezed her. "The one thing I'm sure of is the sex. I'll do, or not do, whatever you need." She smiled, unable to resist the tease. "Even if it makes you blush."

"Can people really find happiness after a week together in Vegas?" Cori murmured.

Rae kissed her. "I have no idea, but we're going to find out."

Cori examined Rae's bedroom, taking in the monochrome prints on the walls. A pond at sunrise, battered dock extending into the water. The Hoover Dam looming high overhead, water spilling out racing toward the photographer. A bullfighting arena, sun streaking in the arched entry over a bull, proud and wide, its head down and foot stomping, ready to charge.

She let her gaze roam past a deep mahogany chest of drawers to the three-wick candle on the side table next to the platform bed. Her eyes tracked from item to item, taking stock, cataloguing, studiously avoiding Rae. The room, the reflective choices of artwork, the generous amount of framed photos of Norma and Rae, the clean lines of the furniture, were at odds with the den of iniquity Cori had expected to find. Rae's aggressive pursuit of sex was not evidenced here.

Rae stepped into view, gathering Cori's hands in hers. "You okay?"

Cori nodded. "This isn't what I expected."

"Really?" Rae tilted her head. "What did you expect?"

"I don't know…not this."

Rae regarded her, but didn't respond.

"Fine." Cori gave in. "Mirrors on the ceiling? Plush

velvet blankets on a giant round bed? A full array of sex toys on display in a glass case?"

Rae's eyebrows edged higher with each sentence. "Cori, I had no idea you were such a freak." She shook her head and made a tsking sound. "That's not really my style, but we can redecorate if you want."

Cori pulled her into a hug, laughing. She held her longer than she intended, her laughter fading to amazement. This was happening. She was here with Rae, in Rae's apartment, her bedroom, and Rae was saying all the right things, offering everything Cori wanted. She squeezed Rae tighter. Rae lowered her hands to Cori's waist, her fingers massaging a comforting, possessive tattoo through the thin cotton of Cori's T-shirt.

"Let me help with that." Cori pulled the shirt over her head, inviting Rae to explore skin instead of fabric. "Okay?"

Rae's movements were small and lazy, but persistent. A shiver started around Cori's thighs and worked its way through her body, raising a trail of bumps across her waist and chest. Rae tightened her hold, her gaze intense and possessive. Cori melted, her belly burning with need. Rae's touch laid claim to her, establishing ownership, from the press of her lips to her tongue pushing in and her palms moving out, flattening against Cori's back and pulling her close. Each caress was full of promise. Every kiss a declaration of intent, and not just for the moment.

Something had changed. Rae was looking at her with a quiet confidence Cori had never seen. She stared back and relaxed in Rae's arms, opening her lips, her soul, to the hot, wet invading demand. She wormed her arms up under Rae's shirt and grasped her shoulders, digging her fingers in, nails scratching, marking her territory. Rae's moan reverberated inside Cori's mouth.

"I need," she gasped between Rae's kisses, her words swallowed, lapped up by Rae's tongue. "Naked...you... please."

Cori tugged Rae's shirt off, slick skin-on-skin her driving focus. She thanked the goddess that Rae was not wearing a bra. She lifted her mouth away from Rae's and sucked Rae's hard nipple, tugging sharply with her teeth.

"God," Rae pleaded.

Rae's hands slid lower and cupped her ass. Cori cursed her jeans and sucked harder. Rae jerked her up, forcing Cori's legs around her waist, and carried her to the bed. She dropped Cori none too gently, and yanked off the rest of her own clothes, stumbling as she tried unsuccessfully to pull her booted foot through her pant leg.

"Dammit." She collapsed on the floor in a heap, fingers scratching at her laces.

Cori laughed. Affection, tinged with longing, settled in her heart. Rae brought all the right emotions to life in her. Lust, longing, hope, anticipation, and happiness.

"Why are you laughing?" Rae waved her finger at Cori's Levi's and satin bra, her voice mocking and stern. "Make yourself useful. Take those off."

"Yes, ma'am." Cori thrilled at the command as she hurried off with her clothes.

Rae, newly naked, stood at the edge of the bed, her hands raised, a breath away from touching Cori. "You're beautiful." She cupped Cori's breasts, massaging her nipples with her thumbs, light and soft. "Perfect."

Cori lowered herself, drawing Rae with her. She explored the tan lines on Rae's hips, getting to know her again. This slow, sometimes playful, sometimes urgent, dance was pushing her to her limits. She wanted Rae's mouth on her. Now. She spread her legs and pulled Rae's hips into the vee, arching at the half-touch where she wanted Rae the most.

"Please, Rae."

"Please?" Rae teased.

Cori circled her hips, inviting, urging. "Yes, please."

Rae pushed back, pinning Cori to the bed with her weight, holding her still. "Wait…please…just let me enjoy you." The laughter in her eyes vanished. Her voice was suddenly serious. She moved her hand lower, smoothing over Cori's belly, fingers teasing the tight curls at the apex of Cori's legs. "I thought you were gone, that I'd lost you forever. I need," she slid her fingers into Cori, slow and certain, "this."

"Yes." Cori held herself rigid, her body aching to move, to force Rae's fingers in faster, harder. She felt Rae, this time the pulsing heat and the perfection of being filled. Rae flexed inside her, moving deeper, pulling out, easing in again, more this time. Wider. Stretching her. The rumbling storm in her belly swept up, threatening to overtake her.

"Stay with me, Cori." Rae stared down at her in rapt concentration, beads of sweat pooling on her brow.

Cori clutched at her, holding Rae's hips tight to her with Rae's hand between their bodies, Rae's fingers inside her. Rae moved her hips, pulling back, thrusting forward, pumping through Cori, pushing her higher. Rae had asked her to wait, to hold back, to make it last, but it was too good, too much. Rae braced herself on one trembling arm as she drove Cori toward release, the heavy weight of her body grounding Cori, keeping her from flying off into the stratosphere.

She lifted her hips, rising to meet Rae, again, again, again, matching Rae's rhythm. First slow, then fast, then slow again, barely moving, torturing Cori. Cori drew tighter, impossibly tighter. Her orgasm threatened to overtake her, to drown her. "Please." She thrashed her head, unable to hold back. "Please."

Rae captured her mouth, pushing into her with her tongue, filling her, smothering her cries. "Now, Cori." She thrust harder, her thumb gliding across Cori's clit, pushing it flat, circling. "Come for me now."

Permission. All the lights in Vegas crashed through her, colliding and exploding. The overwhelming climax was Rae's gift to her. The trembling, whimpering, begging, wreck of mess she collapsed into was the woman Rae made of her.

When the room came back by slow degrees, Rae was hovering over her, smiling and cocky. Cori pulled her down in a tight hug and kissed her, intent on communicating her essence, her hopes, her emotions. Rae belonged to her. Everything else would take care of itself.

"I'm so glad you opened the door," Cori said.

Rae gathered her closer and pressed a kiss to her temple. "Me, too."

Cori didn't know all the answers. Didn't know what the future promised, but this was one gamble she had to take. Win or lose, she was all in.

About the Author

Jove Belle grew up in southern Idaho and now lives in Portland, Oregon, with her partner of thirteen years. When she's not writing, Jove dedicates her time to chasing her four-year-old around the house, making silly faces at the baby, and being generally grateful for the crazy carnival ride of life.

Her other works include the romantic intrigue novel *Edge of Darkness* (Bold Strokes 2008) and the forthcoming romance *Chaps*.

Books Available From Bold Strokes Books

truelesbianlove.com by Carsen Taite. Mackenzie Lewis and Dr. Jordan Wagner have very different ideas about love, but discover truelesbianlove is closer than a click away. (978-1-60282-071-5)

Justice at Risk by John Morgan Wilson. Benjamin Justice's blind date leads to a rare opportunity for legitimate work, but a reckless risk changes his life forever. (978-1-60282-059-3)

Run to Me by Lisa Girolami. Burned by the four-letter word called love, the only thing Beth Standish wants to do is run for—or maybe from—her life. (978-1-60282-034-0)

Split the Aces by Jove Belle. In the neon glare of Sin City, two women ride a wave of passion that threatens to consume them in a world of fast money and fast times. (978-1-60282-033-3)

Uncharted Passage by Julie Cannon. Two women on a vacation that turns deadly face down one of nature's most ruthless killers—and find themselves falling in love. (978-1-60282-032-6)

Night Call by Radclyffe. All medevac helicopter pilot Jett McNally wants to do is fly and forget about the horror and heartbreak she left behind in the Middle East, but anesthesiologist Tristan Holmes has other plans. (978-1-60282-031-9)

Lake Effect Snow by C.P. Rowlands. News correspondent Annie T. Booker and FBI Agent Sarah Moore struggle to stay one step ahead of disaster as Annie's life becomes the war zone she once reported on. Eclipse EBook (978-1-60282-068-5)

Revision of Justice by John Morgan Wilson. Murder shifts into high gear, propelling Benjamin Justice into a raging fire that consumes the Hollywood Hills, burning steadily toward the famous Hollywood Sign—and the identity of a cold-blooded killer. Gay Mystery. (978-1-60282-058-6)

I Dare You by Larkin Rose. Stripper by night, corporate raider by day, Kelsey's only looking for sex and power, until she meets a woman who stirs her heart and her body. (978-1-60282-030-2)

Truth Behind the Mask by Lesley Davis. Erith Baylor is drawn to Sentinel Pagan Osborne's quiet strength, but the secrets between them strain duty and family ties. (978-1-60282-029-6)

Cooper's Deale by KI Thompson. Two would-be lovers and a decidedly inopportune murder spell trouble for Addy Cooper, no matter which way the cards fall. (978-1-60282-028-9)

Romantic Interludes 1: Discovery ed. by Radclyffe and Stacia Seaman. An anthology of sensual, erotic contemporary love stories from the best-selling Bold Strokes authors. (978-1-60282-027-2)

A Guarded Heart by Jennifer Fulton. The last place FBI Special Agent Pat Roussel expects to find herself is assigned to an illicit private security gig baby-sitting a celebrity. (Ebook) (978-1-60282-067-8)

Saving Grace by Jennifer Fulton. Champion swimmer Dawn Beaumont, injured in a car crash she caused, flees to Moon Island, where scientist Grace Ramsay welcomes her. (Ebook) (978-1-60282-066-1)

The Sacred Shore by Jennifer Fulton. Successful tech industry survivor Merris Randall does not believe in love at first sight until she meets Olivia Pearce. (Ebook) (978-1-60282-065-4)

Passion Bay by Jennifer Fulton. Two women from different ends of the earth meet in paradise. Author's expanded edition. (Ebook) (978-1-60282-064-7)

Never Wake by Gabrielle Goldsby. After a brutal attack, Emma Webster becomes a self-sentenced prisoner inside her condo—until the world outside her window goes silent. (Ebook) (978-1-60282-063-0)

The Caretaker's Daughter by Gabrielle Goldsby. Against the backdrop of a nineteenth-century English country estate, two women struggle to find love. (Ebook) (978-1-60282-062-3)

Simple Justice by John Morgan Wilson. When a pretty-boy cokehead is murdered, former LA reporter Benjamin Justice and his reluctant new partner, Alexandra Templeton, must unveil the real killer. (978-1-60282-057-9)

Remember Tomorrow by Gabrielle Goldsby. Cees Bannigan and Arieanna Simon find that a successful relationship rests in remembering the mistakes of the past. (978-1-60282-026-5)

Put Away Wet by Susan Smith. Jocelyn "Joey" Fellows has just been savagely dumped—when she posts an online personal ad, she discovers more than just the great sex she expected. (978-1-60282-025-8)

Homecoming by Nell Stark. Sarah Storm loses everything that matters—family, future dreams, and love—will her new "straight" roommate cause Sarah to take a chance at happiness? (978-1-60282-024-1)

The Three by Meghan O'Brien. A daring, provocative exploration of love and sexuality. Two lovers, Elin and Kael, struggle to survive in a postapocalyptic world. (Ebook) (978-1-60282-056-2)

Falling Star by Gill McKnight. Solley Rayner hopes a few weeks with her family will help heal her shattered dreams, but she hasn't counted on meeting a woman who stirs her heart. (978-1-60282-023-4)

Lethal Affairs by Kim Baldwin and Xenia Alexiou. Elite operative Domino is no stranger to peril, but her investigation of journalist Hayley Ward will test more than her skills. (978-1-60282-022-7)

A Place to Rest by Erin Dutton. Sawyer Drake doesn't know what she wants from life until she meets Jori Diamantina—only trouble is, Jori doesn't seem to share her desire. (978-1-60282-021-0)

Warrior's Valor by Gun Brooke. Dwyn Izsontro and Emeron D'Artansis must put aside personal animosity and unwelcome attraction to defeat an enemy of the Protector of the Realm. (978-1-60282-020-3)

Finding Home by Georgia Beers. Take two polar-opposite women with an attraction for one another they're trying desperately to ignore, throw in a far-too-observant dog, and then sit back and enjoy the romance. (978-1-60282-019-7)

Word of Honor by Radclyffe. All Secret Service Agent Cameron Roberts and First Daughter Blair Powell want is a small intimate wedding, but the paparazzi and a domestic terrorist have other plans. (978-1-60282-018-0)